HUDA AND ME

H. Hayek

ALLEN&UNWIN
SYDNEY • MELBOURNE • AUCKLAND • LONDON

First published by Allen & Unwin in 2021

Allen & Unwin
83 Alexander Street
Crows Nest NSW 2065
Australia
Phone: (61 2) 8425 0100
Email: info@allenandunwin.com
Web: www.allenandunwin.com

 A catalogue record for this book is available from the National Library of Australia

ISBN 978 1 76052 602 3

For teaching resources, explore www.allenandunwin.com/resources/for-teachers

Cover and text design by Debra Billson
Cover and text images: girl & boy © Shutterstock/pikepicture; departures board © Shutterstock/ Hywit Dimyadi; benches & plane © Shutterstock/ ProStockStudio; suitcases © Shutterstock/ MuchMania; houses, clouds & trees © Shutterstock/ jenny on the moon
Author photo by Radiant Studio
Set in 11/17 pt Sabon by Midland Typesetters, Australia
This book was printed in March 2021 in Australia by McPherson's Printing Group

10 9 8 7 6 5 4 3 2

hhayek.com

For my mama and baba. For my boys.
Love you forever.
Little Pigeon, you were my backbone.

The Airport

She's sitting in the airport lounge, fiddling with our tickets. I can tell she's excited because she has a little smile on her face and she keeps glancing at her pink digital watch. I can't believe we're doing this. I can't believe we're running away from home. Well, we're not really running away. We'll come back. We're running to our parents. On the other side of the world. We're getting out of Melbourne, because it all became too much. At least for Huda. And I'm an idiot for agreeing to go with her. But I need to make sure she doesn't do anything stupid, or get herself into some kind of mess.

We'll be dead meat if we're caught before we reach Lebanon. We'll be in trouble with Aunt Amel, with our principal and with the police. Not to mention what Mum and Dad will do if they find out before we can explain. Thinking about it now makes me nervous. I check the time on my watch. Fifteen minutes until boarding.

Huda's looking at the red tag around her neck, trying to read the words. I can see her lips moving as she sounds out the letters.

'Akeal,' she calls to me, more loudly than she needs to. She's sitting with her legs crossed on the fancy purple couch opposite me, like she's watching telly at home. Her school backpack is on the floor next to her, half open. Two dolls' heads poke out. I told her not to pack any toys. 'What's un-accompeed minor mean?'

Un-accompeed. I want to tell her it means someone who goes to pee without help.

'It means you don't have an adult with you,' I say, shaking my head.

She looks at me with her black eyes and smiles. A naughty smile. She knows her plan is going perfectly. Huda might not be the smartest kid in her class, but I don't know any other nine-year-old who would steal a credit card and convince an airline to let her fly to the other side of the world.

As I sigh at my little sister, the announcement is made: 'All children travelling on flight XFL60 to Lebanon, please board at the gate now.'

Huda grins. She grabs her bag and zips it shut. Then she pulls her crumpled plane ticket from her pocket and tries to smooth the creases from it. She looks at me, still smiling. I want to stick my fingers in her dimples and see how deep they'll go.

'Are you ready, brother?'

In a way, she says the word *brother* to tease me, but I know she's also reminding me that I have to stay with her because she's two years younger than me.

'I guess so. Let's see if they actually let us on this plane.'

Huda doesn't wait for me while I pull my own plane ticket out of my pocket. In the flash of an eye, she's in the queue with the other kids waiting to board. The problem is, all those kids are with their parents. You might even think Huda was part of someone's family, the way she's standing there looking around with such excitement on that round, chubby face.

I catch up to her and she whispers in my ear, 'Almost there, Akeal, almost there.' She giggles, but I feel like wetting myself.

The queue moves slowly. Tickets are scanned, passports double-checked, and then, one by one, families disappear behind the glass doors to get onto the plane. I notice two security guards standing a few metres away, and my fingers clench around the straps of my backpack.

3

I want to spew. My back is sweaty and my singlet clings to my skin. We're going to be arrested, I know it.

'You look green, Akeal,' says Huda. She's scrunching up her face like she's grossed out by me. 'If you keep breathing like that, you're gonna faint. I'm too small to pick you up off the floor.'

I want to tell her we're going to one of those jails for children. The ones where we only get to see our parents once a month, and where we have to shovel horse poo for eight hours a day and eat homebrand cornflakes with no sugar every single day for breakfast. Instead, I stare at the patterned tiles on the floor and swallow hard.

Huda's still looking at me in disgust as we get to the front of the line and I finally pull my gaze from the floor. I see a woman smiling at us. She's wearing bright-red lipstick and has a hanky tied around her neck.

'Ah, unaccompanied minors. Boarding passes, please.' I can see now that she's fake-smiling. She has a little smear of red lipstick on her front tooth.

'Here you go, miss,' says Huda, handing over her ticket. She grabs mine from my sweaty palm and passes it over too.

Red Tooth analyses our boarding passes. Her eyes narrow. She doesn't scan our tickets.

Huda shoots me a look and purses her lips together. Her left cheek twitches.

'Passports, please.'

Huda nods and hands them to the woman quickly. Red Tooth opens my passport to the photo page, looks at my picture, and then looks at me. She turns to Huda, opens her passport, looks at her too, then raises her eyebrows.

This is all my fault. I wish I stopped Huda from taking Aunt Amel's credit card. I wish I stopped her from booking the tickets on the internet. I should've known better. I knew we'd get caught.

'Step to the side, please, children,' says Red Tooth. She's not smiling anymore. She gestures to the security guards to come over. They stand on either side of us.

'What's wrong, miss?' Huda asks. I know she's trying to sound bubbly. It's the voice she uses just before she bursts into tears.

'Standard protocol, dear. We need to call your parents to make sure you're okay to fly.'

'Oh, you don't need to do that, miss. They're the ones who booked us these tickets. Because they miss us so much.'

'Yes, little girl. But we need to make sure just one last time that your parents have given permission for you to travel today.'

Huda bites her lip. Her dimples are gone.

My stomach cramps. I can feel puke in my throat. My sister looks at me. Her lips are turned down and her eyes are watery.

We're dead.

Party's Over

The disaster all started a week ago. It was Mr Kostiki's birthday, and everything seemed normal enough. Huda spent the day with Mr Kostiki, looking at his coin collection and eating tinned sardines, and then came home to help Mum bake his birthday cake. Mum and Dad don't celebrate birthdays, but they think Mr Kostiki is a nice old man, and he's also Huda's best friend, so they didn't want him to be alone on his special day.

Mr Kostiki came for dinner, and after our first course, he asked my eldest brother Omar to put on some special Polish music in his honour. He then rather unexpectedly jumped onto the big coffee table in the middle of our family room and showed all us seven kids how to Polish dance.

'What you really need to do, children, is to bend the knees nice and tight, then spring up like you're a jack-in-the-box!' Mr Kostiki shouted. Then he bobbed all the way down until he was almost squatting on the table and jumped back up.

I'd never seen him move that fast. This was also the first time I'd ever seen Mr Kostiki belly laugh. Usually he only chuckles softly at Huda's weird ideas or jokes about chickens.

Omar used Mum's phone to find a clip of traditional Polish dancers, where all the men wore cool belts and held long axes. The women in the video wore flowery dresses and had red bows in their hair. Huda pretended to be like them, twirling around the coffee table. She looked as if she was in her own world, probably imagining she was in Poland a hundred years ago.

Omar held up the phone so Huda could copy the dancers. He might be seventeen and look almost like a grown-up, with wispy man-hair on his face, but I know he likes to spend time with us – even though he says we're annoying.

My big sister Kholoud grabbed Mr Kostiki a long wooden spoon from the kitchen drawer, so he could pretend it was an axe to dance with. This made him even happier and gave him even more energy to spring about on the tabletop.

Kholoud stood by the couch, clapping along to the Polish tune, her fluoro-yellow nail polish and silver nose-stud sparkling under the lampshade. I knew she was too embarrassed to dance with us – she'd be thinking about what her friends in Year 10 would say – but I grabbed her hand and copied Mr Kostiki's moves anyway. Kholoud rolled her eyes at me and flopped her arms along as I hopped around her.

Mum and Dad watched from the kitchen, laughing. Mum was finishing the last of the icing on Mr Kostiki's cake and Dad was putting three mugs of coffee, two red and one brown, on Mum's favourite serving tray – the brass one with the olden-day swirly Arabic patterns. I can trace my fingers over those patterns for hours and forever be surprised by how tricky but perfect the design is. Dad carried the tray over into the family room but realised he had nowhere to put it, with dancing kids everywhere and Mr Kostiki puffing away on the coffee table.

I thought Dad might start dancing with us too, until the twins started grabbing at his legs while they did their own strange disco floor routine around him. Dad struggled to keep the tray balanced and the steaming coffee from spilling all over them.

Suha and Layla never seem to notice when there's danger. They don't look the same, but they're like exact copies of each other on the inside. They both read at least three novels a week and score equal highest marks in their classes for every test. They're only a year and a half older than me, but they think me and Huda are 'undeveloped'.

I know that because I heard them tell Mum once. But I also remember what Mum said back to them in a low voice as I eavesdropped from the next room: *Girls, you mark my words, Huda and Akeal have a bond like no one else in the family. One day we're all going see how, together, they're unstoppable.*

Mum finished icing the cake and added some rainbow candles. I didn't think there were more than ten and wondered if Mr Kostiki would be offended. Mum stood at the kitchen bench beaming at us all, like she was watching the very end of a movie – the best part, where all the characters have got everything they wanted and their lives are going to be wonderful.

If we only knew.

Mum swept over to baby Raheed in his walker, his rosy cheeks brighter than normal as he slapped his hands together to the music, a bit of baby drool running down his chin onto his super-cute jumpsuit. As Mum pulled him up towards her, his little feet caught on the walker seat, and he wriggled his chubby legs until he was free and in Mum's arms. The music finished and the room went quiet, except for our giggles.

'Put on another one, old boy!' Mr Kostiki shouted to Omar, even though Omar was standing right beside him. Mr Kostiki's face was red and he was panting. He was smiling but frowning at the same time, almost like he was in pain. He grabbed Omar's shoulder to stop himself from falling off the table.

'How about some cake now, Jozef?' said Mum.

'Very well, very well.' Mr Kostiki sounded annoyed but took Omar's hands and climbed off the coffee table, then slumped onto the couch. Huda jumped to sit next to him and started touching the silky cravat under his neck while they waited for the cake.

When Mr Kostiki first moved next door, me and Huda would stare at him from the window. We didn't know why he was always wearing colourful silky tissue things in his shirt collar. Huda guessed it was so he could quickly wipe his nose without having to use his hands. But after Huda became friends with him, he told her they're called cravats and he wears them to look important.

Mr Kostiki brushed Huda's hand away. 'Aghh, leave it, little Huda. I'll give you one to play with tomorrow.'

Dad placed the brass tray on the coffee table, among some new shoeprints, and handed the brown mug to Mr Kostiki.

'Ahh, my special mug,' said Mr Kostiki. 'Half a teaspoon of sugar?'

Dad nodded.

Mum passed baby Raheed over to Suha and went to get the cake. Suha muttered something under her breath about babies taking years to grow up, and Layla nodded in knowing agreement. Mum placed the big green cake next to the brass tray and Mr Kostiki took one last sip of coffee, sat up straight, and put his hands in his lap. This was his moment and he knew it.

Huda was practically shaking with excitement, the smile on her face even bigger than Mr Kostiki's. I turned off the lamp so the candles could sparkle in the dark.

After we'd all had our cake, and Suha and Layla had made us cups of mint tea, Mum said there was something she needed to tell us. I think Mr Kostiki had dozed off because his eyes were closed, even though he was still sitting upright with his plate on his lap.

She bit her lip and looked around the room at each of us. 'Kids, we're going to Lebanon.'

I couldn't believe my ears. *Finally*, we were going to meet my parents' parents! And we'd be able to see real-life snow, and the humungous rock sticking out of the ocean that's on all the postcards.

Huda jumped off the couch and fist-pumped the air. I gave her a high-five, and Omar picked Raheed up off the floor and spun him in the air. Kholoud grinned – I had forgotten she even had teeth. Suha and Layla chuckled and held hands.

Mum and Dad looked at each other, but they didn't seem happy like we were. Dad cleared his throat.

'Ah, what your mum means is *we're* going to Lebanon.' He pointed to himself and then at Mum, then back to himself and then at Mum again. In case we didn't get it, he then said, 'Us. Just the two of us.'

My eyes blinked a few times on their own and I felt my breathing get quicker. It was like my brain was trying to tell the rest of my body what it had just heard.

I glanced around at my brothers and sisters. Raheed pulled his thumb out of his mouth and stared open-mouthed at Omar.

'So... we're staying here? While you go to Lebanon?' I wasn't sure if it was Suha or Layla who'd asked.

'Yes, that's right,' Mum said. She glanced down at her hands, rubbing them together.

At that moment, all us kids jumped up from our seats and cheered. Even Raheed bobbed his cute bum up and down in Omar's arms, drool running like melted ice over Omar's shirt.

No parents. Only us kids. With Mr Kostiki next door. Coco Pops three meals a day. This was even better than a holiday to Lebanon.

Mr Kostiki's eyes jerked open and he jolted up from the couch, looking confused about where he was and what was happening.

This time Mum had to raise her voice. 'Ya wlad! Kids! Sit!' She'd stopped rubbing her hands together but still had that look on her face. 'Your dad and I aren't going for a holiday. We are going because my mum is very sick.'

My heart sank.

'You know we've been saving for years hoping we could all go as a family, but my mum needs me to care for her now. And...'

She looked at Dad, like she was asking him to finish her sentence.

'And Aunt Amel will be babysitting you.' Dad said it quickly, and then his eyes darted to the floor.

We all knew what that meant. The party was over.

The Aeroplane

Red Tooth goes into an office with a clear glass door. She's taken our passports and tickets with her. She taps at the computer. Then she picks up the phone and dials.

'I'm sorry, Akeal,' Huda whispers.

I'm praying there'll be no answer. That the phone will ring out. That maybe all the phone lines will be busy by some miracle. I feel like getting out my prayer mat and putting my head on the floor right there and then. Oh God, please don't let it all end here.

The line connects and Red Tooth taps her pen on the desk as she talks, never taking her eyes off us. One of the security guards has his hand on his belt buckle – he's getting ready to take out his handcuffs. Finally Red Tooth hangs up the phone. Her heels clicking on the tiles sound louder and louder as she closes in.

This is what dead meat feels like.

When she starts talking, I'm so anxious I can barely understand what she's saying. Huda grabs my hand and holds it tight. I can't remember the last time she held my hand.

'You must be very careful not to' – I vomit in my mouth a little. I don't want to go to prison – 'trip on the step as you board the plane.'

She scans our tickets and hands them back to us with our passports. Then she points to her name tag.

'My name is Rosetta. If you need anything throughout the flight, please let me or one of the flight crew know. Have an enjoyable trip.' She smiles.

'Thank you very much, Miss Rosetta.' Huda releases my hand and grins. She skips ahead to board the plane.

I don't understand what's just happened. How did we get away with it?

I hurry after Huda, who grabs three headsets from a tub in the winding corridor leading to the aeroplane. 'They're free!' she shouts, waving them over her shoulder without looking back. I whisper to God, making a special prayer that we will get to Lebanon safely. By the time I reach the plane doors, Huda is annoyed.

'Take your time, why don't you?'

15

'I was praying. You should too.'

'Already did.'

I don't believe her but I'm too tired to argue.

'Anyway, let's get out of this dump and go see Mum and Dad,' she says.

The plane is huge. There are rows of two seats against the windows on both sides, plus a row of four seats in the middle.

Most people are already seated, and as we walk towards our row at the back of the plane Huda smiles at the people she passes. Even though her hair hasn't been brushed in a couple of days and she slept in the clothes she's wearing, people think she's adorable. I can tell from the way they smile at her and then at each other.

As if to prove me right, a woman with straight black hair, big eyes and tiny eyebrows clutches Huda's wrist as she walks ahead in front of me. 'Are you two sweethearts travelling alone?'

The woman is around Mum's age. The man she's with stops reading his book and peeks at us through his thick-framed glasses.

Huda nods slowly, like a sad orphan. 'Yes, we're unaccompeed minors,' she says in a glum voice.

The woman makes a small whimpering sound and puts her palm on her cheek. She and her partner look at each other, smiling, but with pretend sad eyes. 'Well, you just let us know if you need anything. We're right here. You be brave, okay?'

Huda tilts her head to the side and nods. 'Thank you,' she sniffs and continues to shuffle down the aisle. I can tell the woman and her partner wish they could wrap my sister up and take her home.

We find our row, and Huda takes the spot near the window. We stuff our backpacks under the seats in front of us, then Huda looks past me to the middle row next to us and grins. 'Look, Akeal, it's that Muslim grandma.'

She's referring to a frail, hunched-over nun sitting alone in the middle of the four seats across from us. 'She's a nun, Huda,' I say.

'Wow, a Muslim nun!'

'No, she's not Muslim. That's a habit on her head.' I remember back to my World Religions class last year.

'What kind of habit does she have? Does she always scratch or something?'

Huda smiles at me cheekily as the old woman turns slowly and looks at us. Huda mouths the words 'As Salamu Alaykum' to her and puts her hands on her chest, like she's seen older people do at the mosque.

I shake my head at my sister, but the old woman just smiles back. I'm about to try to explain to Huda again what a nun is when a man with a whole tub of gel in his hair comes towards us. His white shirt is so bright and crisp I think it could be made from printer paper. He squats down beside our seats.

'I'm your flight attendant today,' he says in a squeaky voice. 'My name is Martin.' He glances at his notebook. 'And you must be Hooda and Akeaw.'

Huda snorts and tries to muffle a laugh at the way he pronounced our names.

'Now, Hooda and Akeaw, make sure you buckle your seatbelts nice and tight. If you need anything today, you just press that button and I'll come right over.' He points to a little button with a lightbulb on it built into my seat's armrest. 'Can I do anything for you before we begin the safety briefing?'

I open my mouth to say no and thank you, but Huda cuts in before me. 'Thanks very much, Martin. I'd like a Coke, please.'

Martin's eyes widen for a brief moment. 'Sure, just make sure you finish it before take-off, okay little lady?'

'Actually, Martin, make it two Cokes. My brother needs a drink. And do you have any of those kids' colouring packs? I'd like one of those too, please.'

I glare at Huda.

'Two Cokes and a colouring pack coming right up,' Martin says before heading off down the aisle.

'You can't just go around demanding things like that, Huda,' I say.

'I wasn't demanding. He asked if I wanted anything. You need to relax, brother.'

'Relax! We were almost just sent to a kids' prison for the rest of our lives!'

Martin brings us our drinks and Huda's colouring pack and we fall silent until he leaves again.

'I don't know how Mum and Dad agreed to let us onto this plane when that woman called them,' I hiss when it's safe to talk again.

'It wasn't Mum and Dad on the phone,' says Huda casually, as she takes a sip of Coke.

I pause for a moment. 'What do you mean it wasn't Mum and Dad?'

'It wasn't them,' she says, taking another sip.

'Huda, for heaven's sake, what are you on about?'

'I gave 'em Mr Kostiki's number when I booked online. It asked for parent or garden details, so I typed in his address and phone number.'

I'm guessing she means *guardian*.

'You don't think I'd really give 'em Mum and Dad's number, do you? Even a child wouldn't do that.'

I don't know whether to laugh or cry. 'And Mr Kostiki went *along* with it? When the airline rang him out of the blue?'

Huda reclines her seat. 'Mr Kostiki has a lot of faith in me, *Akeaw*. You really need to take a chill pill.' She taps her watch. 'And look, no one else will realise we're missing until after school, in another five or six hours, and we'll be out of Australia and in the air by then. So just calm down and don't give us away before the plane takes off, okay?'

As much as I hate to admit it, she's right. I can't believe we actually got onto the plane, and that we're on our way to Mum and Dad. Surely the worst of it's over. I need to relax.

I take a sip of my Coke, put on my earphones, and look past Huda out the window. Martin finishes pointing to the emergency exits and winds up his safety briefing, then straps himself into his special seat at the front of the plane.

This is it. We can finally put the last week of torture behind us. As the plane rumbles and charges forward, gaining speed on the runway, I can't help but think back to how this all began. The plane lifts itself into the sky. Home seems so far away already.

Mum and Dad Leave

Two nights after Mr Kostiki's birthday party, Mum and Dad left. It's hard to think about it because I miss them so much.

It was only last Sunday, after our last family dinner together. Mum was in her room packing two gigantic red suitcases. There were a lot of gifts for her family: cardigans for her sisters, expensive chocolates for her nieces and nephews, and even creams and medicines from the pharmacy for her sick mum.

Huda was in Mum's walk-in wardrobe, wearing a pair of high heels that were about eight sizes too big for her and throwing clothes around, being 'helpful'.

'This is so pretty, Mum. You have to wear this when

you get there,' said Huda, popping her head out of the wardrobe and holding up a green, sequinned outfit. It was Mum's engagement dress.

Mum smiled and kept packing. She had tears in her eyes.

Huda disappeared into the wardrobe again and I gave Mum a big hug. She always smells like fresh roses. She hugged me back and then bent down so we were eye-level. 'I'll miss you, habibi,' she whispered.

'I'll miss you, Mama.' I could feel tears pricking my eyes too.

'You need to look after her, you know that.' Mum tilted her head towards the wardrobe, where Huda was still making a mess.

'I know, Mama.'

'You're a big boy now. I know you'll make sure she's okay.'

'I will. I promise.'

Huda poked her head out again, this time holding up a black lacy top. 'This one, Mum! You have to wear this one!' When she saw us cuddling, she charged over and threw her arms around Mum too. 'I'm going to miss you more! More than him!'

Mum held us both tight until Dad came in carrying baby Raheed in his arms. Dad kissed him on his rosy cheek and his forehead, then the jiggly soft bit under his chin – everyone's favourite spot. Raheed twisted and turned when he saw us, trying to get to the floor.

'We're only going for two weeks, you monkeys,' Dad said. 'You'll be eating your mum's Lebanese bread and hummus again before you know it.' He half-dropped Raheed onto the carpet. I knew he was trying to cheer us up.

I joined in the joke, because I knew I was a minute away from exploding like a huge tear-bubble. 'Nah, I can't wait for the tabouli!'

Huda rubbed her tummy and smacked her lips together, and I grabbed Raheed and gave him a cuddle. His warm squishy body always makes me feel better. Mum put a last couple of things into the suitcases and zipped them shut just as the twins walked into the bedroom.

'Now listen, kids,' started Mum, 'you all need to show Aunt Amel your best manners. She'll be a guest in our home, and she's doing us a big favour by staying here for two weeks.'

'Why do we need to call her Aunty when she's not our real aunt?' Layla asked, even though she already knew the answer.

'I've told you before,' Mum said, 'it's about respecting those who are older than us.'

The twins rolled their eyes and nodded. Huda stuck out her tongue and put her finger in her mouth, to make out that she was about to spew.

'Enough of that, Huda. I don't want to hear that you've been cheeky. And remember what I told you, Akeal?' Mum glanced from me to Huda, reminding me of my promise.

'I remember, Mum,' I said.

Mum looked around at the five of us and then clapped her hands. 'Come sit with me, my babies.' She hopped onto her big bed, the perfectly made-up white quilt crumpling, and sat with her legs crossed in the middle.

Huda charged onto the bed first, almost like she was doing a bombie in a swimming pool. The rest of us jumped on too, Raheed still in my arms. Mum had tears in her eyes again.

'Nothing's the same as having your mum and dad with you, I know,' she said. 'But let me tell you something special about Aunt Amel. I met her two years ago at that halaqa class I used to go to. Remember the one on Tuesday nights?'

Huda groaned and leaned backwards. 'Ugh, I hated that class. Dad would cook us mujadara *every* Tuesday, and it always turned out like runny soup filled with tiny lentil pebbles.'

I shuddered, remembering. Mum glanced up at Dad, who was standing by the bedroom door, and grinned. He raised one eyebrow, but didn't comment.

'Yes, well, I know Amel isn't your *favourite* of our friends, but she's always been very kind to me – like a

24

sister, when I have none of my own family here.' Mum's voice trembled.

That made me sad for my mum, but I was glad she felt like she had a sister. I couldn't imagine not having any of my siblings around, even though they can be annoying. Perhaps, I thought, even as annoying as Aunt Amel.

'When Raheed was still a tiny baby, Amel was the one who helped us all through. You didn't know it, but when you were at school and Baba was at work, she'd pick up bags of groceries for me. Then she'd stay to look after Raheed, so that I could rest.'

Mum smiled at Raheed and stroked the fine hair on his head. I raised my eyebrows, wondering if it was Aunt Amel who'd bought us all those donuts and sausage rolls when I was starting Grade 5. We hadn't had them in our lunchboxes before or since.

Aunt Amel has never been like Mum and Dad's other friends. Most of them sit in the fancy lounge room when they visit, with their ankles crossed, drinking from small Arabic coffee cups and talking about their kids' 'superb' exam results.

Whenever Aunt Amel came over, though, she seemed to take up every space, all the time. One minute she'd be sitting on the couch reading with one of the twins, the next she'd be laughing with Mum at the stove, then two seconds after that she'd be pulling out weeds from

25

around the letterbox. For the last two Eids she gave each of us a handmade card, with a poem she'd written inside. *Akeal, you are a star. You like bunnies and you will go far.* I think I'd mentioned to her once that a rabbit on TV was cute.

We liked Aunt Amel, sort of, but we didn't like the idea of her being in charge of our house for two weeks.

'Mother, you know we are capable of looking after ourselves,' Suha said bluntly. 'Aunt Amel just seems a little...'

'...extra.' Layla sniffed and nodded at her twin.

Mum sighed. 'I understand you feel that way, but this is what Dad and I think is best. You are wonderful, clever, helpful kids, but you need an adult here. And besides, it will be nice for Aunt Amel, too – a change of scene. She lives in a tiny apartment. And she loves being around you kids.'

The five of us looked at each other, then back at Mum. Layla opened her mouth to say something, but Dad cut in.

'Your mum is right. Now come on, it's getting late. Akeal, help me with the suitcases.'

I popped Raheed onto Huda's lap and sprang off the bed. Dad and I wheeled the bags out to the family room, where Omar and Kholoud were watching TV. They both think they're so cool because they're in high school, but

Mum and Dad think they should focus more on studying instead of watching TV shows that are too rude for us younger kids.

Omar laughed at whatever he was watching and shoved a handful of chips into his mouth. Kholoud sat on the couch painting another coat of fluoro yellow onto her fingernails. I was about to tell her how ugly they looked when we heard a car pull up in the driveway. A door slammed shut. This was it. Aunt Amel had arrived.

Mum came out of her room holding Raheed, followed by Huda and the twins. I could see that they'd all been crying and was glad I'd got out of there before the waterworks erupted. The doorbell rang and we all froze.

Mum pulled herself together first. She opened the door and stretched out her arms to give Aunt Amel a hug.

I couldn't see Aunt Amel at first because it was dark outside, but then she leaned forward. She was wearing a long yellow dress, with an orange hijab tied loosely around her head. Her ponytail stuck out the back of her scarf and bits of hair poked out of the front, across her forehead. As she hugged Mum, our eyes met. I couldn't help but quickly look at the floor. She gave Mum a kiss on both cheeks and then licked her lips. Gross. She was smiling so much I thought her face might crack.

'Salam, Akeal. Come give me a hug.' As she held out her arms, all her bracelets and jewellery clinked and jingled.

I walked over to her slowly and put my hand out, hoping I could get away with a handshake, but Aunt Amel pulled me into her. She smelled funny. Like onions. And the way she had me wrapped in her arms, it was pitch-black. Her hijab was over my head, and bits of my hair caught in her dangly necklace. I held my breath until she let me go, but just before she did, she whispered in my ear, 'We're going to have a wonderful time together.'

I turned around and saw my brothers and sisters watching in sympathy. Mum gestured for them to all go over and say their salam too. Huda hung back, though.

'No way I'm gonna give her a cuddle. I'd rather eat a dead chicken,' she said from the side of her mouth. I hoped she'd stop talking, worried Aunt Amel might hear, but she kept going. 'You looked like you were gonna suffocate. We thought you were done for.'

Mum glared at Huda, and Huda pretended not to notice. Then in the middle of all the hellos and forced hugs, we heard the sound of another car in the driveway and the beep of a horn. This was the car we'd dreaded even more than Aunt Amel's – it was Mum and Dad's taxi to the airport.

Aunt Amel had been late, and the taxi was early.

I'd thought we'd have more time; that we could've sat down together and had tea and some of Mum's sweet biscuits with the sesame seeds on top. But now they were going.

Omar wheeled the first of the two big suitcases to the front door while Dad took the other. Mum was fast-talking to Aunt Amel, trying to fill her in on all the important things, like bedtimes, and where the money was if we needed it, and what to do if Huda refused to take a bath. Then in a matter of seconds, the taxi-driver beeped the horn again and it was time to say goodbye.

Dad quickly gave each of us a peck on the forehead, trying not to show that he was sad, but I could tell he was from the way his hazel eyes drooped. He was in the taxi before I had a chance to tell him a joke to make him feel better.

Next it was time to say goodbye to Mum. As much as I wanted to be strong, I just couldn't be. There's no one in the world like my mum – no one who can cheer me up on a bad day, or make me feel special and happy and safe all at the same time. That's why I bawled like a baby when she gave me that final long, soft hug.

I breathed my mum in and didn't want to pull away. But the taxi beeped again. She pulled away and held me by the shoulders. I couldn't look at her because I felt so weak for my tears, but then I realised everyone was crying.

I looked into Mum's eyes and I felt pain in the middle part of my chest.

Mum forced herself away and spent a few more moments giving my brothers and sisters hugs and saying her goodbyes. And then she slowly walked out the door.

There was silence except for Huda's sobs. Kholoud held Raheed tight, to stop him crawling after Mum. Omar stared at the door, his arms around Suha and Layla's shoulders. I stood there just hoping Mum would come back.

Aunt Amel walked over to the front door and slammed it shut dramatically. The crash made me jump, and a family photo almost leapt off the wall, then tilted off-centre.

'Tears, tears, tears! Nothing will bring them back! Let's just look forward to two glorious weeks together, children!'

Aunt Amel started gliding around the family room, like one of the Polish dancers on the video from the other night. The bottom of her yellow dress was stained brown, like she'd walked through mud. Huda's sobs grew louder, and the sound made Aunt Amel stop floating around and rush over to my sister. She pulled her grubby dress up to Huda's face and began to wipe away her tears. Then she used it to wipe Huda's nose.

'Oh, Hoodie Boodie! Don't be sad! Mum and Dad will be back soon. You know what always made me feel better when I was unhappy as a child?'

She looked around at all of us with her mouth open and her eyes sparkling expectantly, clearly hoping we'd guess the right answer.

The twins opened their mouths to take a shot, but before they could say anything Aunt Amel cut them off. 'Sleep. Sleep always made me feel better!'

Layla and Suha looked at each other, then back at Aunt Amel.

She pointed her longest finger up to the ceiling, almost like we were part of a marching band. 'Off to bed, now. All of you. Never mind about teeth and flossing and all of that – straight to bed.'

None of us moved. Our bedtime wasn't for another hour.

'Off you go, children! You will be fresh and happy in the morning!'

I wasn't sure that was true, and I could tell my brothers and sisters didn't think so either.

Omar shifted his feet. 'C'mon, let's just get an early night. It will make time go quicker anyway,' he said, shrugging his shoulders.

'Good lad! The voice of reason!' Aunt Amel's voice was high-pitched and loud. 'But before you hop into bed, give me little bitty cutie Raheed. I'll keep him safe and cosy with me.'

And Aunt Amel yanked our baby from Kholoud's arms.

Dubai

I must have fallen asleep. When I wake, my eyes barely have a chance to focus before Huda starts talking.

'What do you think? I look good, don't I?'

She's wearing a pink hijab with brightly coloured diamantes all over it and grinning at her own reflection in a small fold-up mirror.

'I think it'd be good to look like a proper Muslim when we get to Lebanon. I'll blend in with everyone else. And besides, I look super cute in this scarf.'

Still beaming from ear to ear, she tilts her head in different directions to get the best look at herself. She looks like she's about to go to a wedding.

Huda puts down the mirror and twists open her tube of strawberry lip gloss. She smears it on her lips and rubs them together, making squelchy sounds.

'Don't you think you look a bit...fancy?' I say, my eyes trying to adjust to all the sparkles.

'Yes, I do think I look very nice, thank you very much.'

Huda shoves her lip gloss back into the seat pocket in front of her, and I notice she's also coloured in her finger-nails with the textas Martin gave her. In pink, of course. I rub my eyes.

'You've slept for hours, brother. Like a little grizzly in hibernation. I watched three movies and ate four ice-creams while you were asleep. You missed out. But that's okay, they'll be bringing us afternoon tea soon. So far, this trip has been worth every penny.'

Huda's talking really fast, and she's fiddling a lot too.

'Did you get some rest?' I ask, wondering where all this energy has come from.

'Nah, too much fun to be asleep, Akeaw.'

We went to bed at midnight and woke up extra early before pretending to go to school this morning, but Huda looks like she's just risen from a two-day nap. She reaches into her seat pocket again and pulls out an almost empty packet of sugared lollies.

'These are so good. This is my second packet. Want one?'

She shoves two into her mouth and begins to suck all the sugar off them. Now I get it. I shake my head.

'Akeal, where do you think all the poo goes when people flush the toilet on a plane? Reckon there's a hole so it falls straight out?'

I crumple my nose. I don't want to think about passengers' poo falling from the sky.

'That's gross. How do you even think about this stuff?'

My sister shrugs.

'Dunno. I gotta go dunny. Move over.'

She lifts up her tray-table and squeezes past me, deliberately putting her hands on my face as though she's trying to stay balanced. My sister's in one of those annoying moods. She laughs as she walks off down the aisle, flicking her scarf over her shoulder. She wants people to notice her new look.

I lean over and lift the window shade. There's nothing below us but white clouds, spread out forever, like a soft bed carrying us to our parents. Looking at them, I feel a sense of calm. This is the first time I've rested in days, and had time to really think – about what's happened, where we are, and where we're going.

I let myself imagine what's at the end of the clouds. Lebanon. Mum and Dad have always told me how beautiful it is, and how they know I'll love it when I finally get there. How I'll be able to play next to the Litani River, like they did when they were kids, and watch the sea from the mountains.

I close my eyes and I can see it. Maybe I'm only imagining the old photos Mum and Dad have showed me, but it's beautiful. I love how the air feels on my skin, and the way the sun shines on my face. I love the green from the cedar trees, the blue from the summer sky, and the big smiles I know are waiting for me. I wonder why I feel like it's where I belong, when I know Melbourne is home.

My stomach rumbles and I open my eyes. The ache in my guts reminds me that I haven't eaten anything since yesterday afternoon. I'm starving. Hopefully Mum will have made something yummy, like rice and chicken soup, when we get there.

I open my backpack and fumble for the muesli bar and apple rolling around at the bottom, but the rolls of cash we stole get in the way. I don't know exactly how much money we nicked, but it has to be thousands. I quickly grab the snacks, zip up my bag and cram it back under the seat in front of me before anyone sees. To make sure it can't be pulled out easily, I give it a couple of hard kicks.

My stomach rumbles again, and I look at my apple. It's bruised and soft and wrinkled, but Mum told me never to waste food, so I make myself eat it. As I force the mush down my throat, the flight attendant with the red lipstick suddenly pops her face in front of mine, so that we're almost eye to eye. I glance at her badge to remind myself of her name. Rosetta.

'Excuse me, would you like help placing your bag into the overhead locker?'

'Um…no, that's okay. Thank you, though, miss.' I want to keep my parents' money as close to me as possible.

'It will be safer and more comfortable if your bag is placed in the locker,' she says firmly, reaching down to try to tug my backpack from its resting spot.

Panicking, I press my legs forward against my seat to block her, so that her hands can't get a decent grip. She grunts and stands.

'Your bag is protruding into the aisle. Unless you fix it, I will be back to remove it and ensure it's placed in the locker securely.' Miss Rosetta glares at me.

'Okay, miss,' I gulp.

She runs her hand through her hair, then walks back towards the front of the plane. I unclip my seatbelt and kick my bag in a little more from the aisle, to make sure it's not sticking out. I wonder for a second if Miss Rosetta knows about the money. I wonder if that's the real reason she was trying to get my bag.

An announcement over the speaker cuts into my thoughts: 'On behalf of the crew, we'd like to thank you for flying with us. We will shortly be making our descent into Dubai International Airport…'

I barely hear the rest of what the pilot is saying as I stagger back into my seat. My fingers fumble with my seatbelt. *Dubai.* I knew we'd get lost in some other country. I don't even know what country Dubai is in. My heart races and the pressure in my ears builds until it hurts. I knew I shouldn't have let Huda book the tickets. It's my fault for falling asleep and not keeping an eye on things.

My polo shirt feels tight around my neck. As I pull at it to try to get more oxygen down my throat, I see Huda skip up the plane aisle towards me. She's grinning so much that I can see both full rows of her white teeth. The closer she gets, the more my ears ring. My sister slides into her seat and buckles her seatbelt. The words in my head muddle. I feel stupid and angry. Stupid for going along with her plan. Angry for letting myself get into this disaster.

I take a big breath, ready to yell and cry and freak out. Huda has no idea what she's done to us. She's busy pretending to read the in-flight magazine.

'Huda—'

It's the only word that comes out of my mouth before she cuts me off. 'Holiday time, baby!' She does a little dance in her seat.

'Are you serious! Holiday time?' I can't believe she doesn't realise we're about to be stranded, alone, in some country on the other side of the world.

'Yeh, bebe! Dubai, here we come!'

I choke on whatever spit is left in my dry mouth.

She cocks an eyebrow at me. 'What the heck is wrong with you, brother? You look araf. Like, really araf. Like, super, seriously revolting.' She chucks the magazine at me.

My mouth opens and closes a few times before I manage to croak, 'Dubai?'

'Yes, Dubai, you ning-nong. Our stopover.'

I haven't seen Huda this excited since Eid last year. It could be the sugar rush. Though she also keeps saying Dubai is 'the city of gold'. She says she read it on the website when she booked our tickets.

We peer out the window as the plane drifts through the clouds and dreamily glides onto the runway without a bump. The tarmac stretches forever, and there are differently sized planes parked in every direction, with all sorts of coloured logos and swirls on their tails.

'Folks, welcome to Dubai International Airport. Local time is 4:05 p.m. and the temperature is forty degrees. For your safety and comfort, please remain seated with your seatbelt fastened until the captain turns off the *fasten seatbelt* sign…'

I glance towards the front of the plane. Miss Rosetta is unlatching the plane door, and Martin is checking over papers on his brown clipboard. He says something to Miss Rosetta and they both look over at us. Martin smiles as he walks up the aisle towards me and my sister.

Huda doesn't notice because she's too busy watching airport workers zip around the tarmac in bright-yellow buggies. I can almost see the sweat dripping from their foreheads from here.

'Hooda and Akeaw, as you're unaccompanied minors, I'll be escorting you off the plane first.'

'Oooh, VIP service. I like it,' Huda chirps as we unclip our seatbelts.

We grab our bags and follow Martin to the front of the plane, where Miss Rosetta is busy ordering an old man with a walking stick back into his seat. She flicks her head my way and points to my shoes. I think she's going to yell at me for not shifting my feet when she tried to get my backpack earlier.

'Shoelaces. Tie them now. You'll end up falling head-first from the plane.'

I glance down and see that she's right.

'Sheesh, bit of a grump, isn't she?' Huda mumbles under her breath as I bend to tie my laces. Once I'm done, Martin leads us out the door of the aircraft.

I expect to walk straight into the airport but instead find myself at the top of some rickety metal stairs leading down to the tarmac. My head spins at how high up we are. The hot air outside hits me in the face like a cricket bat.

Huda is already three steps ahead of me, and I see a woman standing at the bottom of the steps waiting for us. She's wearing a bright-green uniform that makes her look like a chef, but without the funny hat. Her light-brown hair is twisted into a loose bun and her high heels are taller than any of Mum's.

Before I quite reach the bottom, she's already speaking to my sister. 'Hello, Huda, welcome to Dubai! My name is Amira.'

Amira doesn't hug Huda, but it looks like she wants to, the way her hands are moving around in circles. She speaks loudly and with a lot of good expression – that's how my teacher Mr Morrison would describe it.

Huda turns back to me and winks, then turns back to Amira. 'Thank you very much, Amira. Pleased to meet you, indeed.' She's trying to sound proper.

Amira bows her head softly towards my sister. 'I'm your customer service agent and will be escorting you through Dubai Airport until it's time to board your second flight. You'll be under my care and supervision.'

Huda shoots me another look, but her eyes aren't big and round anymore and her mouth is crumpled to the side. She shifts her eyeballs between me and Amira as if to say, *Did you just hear what this woman said?*

Martin passes Amira the brown clipboard with our papers clipped to it. 'Okay, kids, I'll be seeing you on the next flight in an hour,' he chirps. He ruffles my hair before making his way back up the steps to the plane.

Amira is grinning, like she can't wait to spend the next hour with us. 'After you, children. Let's get out of the heat and into the airport.'

She waves her hand towards two humungous red-and-black buses. A shiny yellow buggy is parked in front of them. The other passengers from our plane start to make their way down the stairs now too – hundreds of them, struggling with their small wheelie suitcases, squinting in the bright light and burning heat. In a minute, we'll be crammed between them all on a bus. I couldn't think of anything worse.

Huda hops onto the bus closest to us, but before I can follow my sister, Amira zips ahead of me.

'Ah, Huda love, we'll be taking that.' Amira points to the yellow buggy.

My sister jiggles a little. 'The cool buggy?'

'Yep!' Amira's green eyes sparkle.

Huda lunges off the bus and before the crowd of other passengers have even hit the bottom of the stairs, we've leapt into the buggy. There's no roof and no air con, but we don't care.

'Seatbelts!' Amira calls from the front seat as she hits the accelerator, barely giving us time to clip ourselves in.

The air is boiling, and strands of Huda's mangled hair poking out of her scarf flick into my eyes. But I don't care. This is what freedom must feel like.

I twist to look at my little sister as her head swings in the opposite direction to one of Amira's sharp turns. Her face is stained with dirt and sweat and sugar, but she laughs – like, really laughs. And hearing Huda giggling next to me like that reminds me that no matter what happens, she will always be my favourite little sister.

The List

'Akealie!'

Aunt Amel's voice shot through my ears. I thought it was the middle of the night at first, because it was still dark. I looked at my alarm clock: 5:02 a.m. She was so close I could feel her sour breath on my face.

'Wake up, little pumpkin! I have an idea! I need you all in the kitchen.' She sounded even more excited than usual.

I didn't move. I didn't want to move. Aunt Amel switched on my lamp and light zapped into my eyes.

'Up and let's go! We have a fabulous day ahead of us!' she shouted and rushed out of my room.

I could hear a fuss happening in the kitchen, so I dragged myself out there to see what was going on. Still in

44

their pyjamas, most of my siblings were already standing in a line in front of the dining table. Huda was the last to join us. She rubbed her half-closed eyes as she walked in. She only had one sock on, and one of her pyjama legs was pulled up to the knee.

'What's going on? Is Mum back?' Huda mumbled.

'Oh no, little Hudie, Mummy isn't back. But I've been up all night thinking of how we can make this a wonderful holiday for me!'

Suha grumbled like a bear.

'Holiday for *you*?' Layla questioned under her breath.

Huda stepped behind me and held the back of my skivvy.

Aunt Amel paced back and forth in front of us. She had Raheed's favourite blue dummy and was tossing it up and down. Mum would've killed us if any one of us had done that. She's always so worried about germs.

'As you know, children,' Aunt Amel began, 'I work at that box factory down on the other side of town. When your mummy told me she was going on holiday, I figured, *Why not! I should take a holiday over here with you kiddies too*. It's not exactly the New Zealand ski trip I've been dying for, nor even the two-day day-spa at Daylesford, but I've always made the best out of any situation...'

None of what Aunt Amel was saying made any sense. She must've realised this from the look on my face.

'What I mean is, I've had to take two weeks off work and this house is so lovely and clean, and you are all so adorable, and your mum is always saying I need to take time to relax a little…'

Huda leaned in closer to me while Aunt Amel was blabbing away. 'What's she talking about, Akeal?' she whispered, her words slurred with exhaustion.

I couldn't answer her, because I still had no idea.

Before any of us could register what was going on, Aunt Amel clicked both her fingers either side of her face and froze.

We all froze too.

She pulled a piece of paper from her pocket.

'This is our pact.'

As she un-scrunched it, I noticed it was covered in doodles.

'From now on, you'll be waking up early. This is good for both of us. Good for you because you know that the greatest blessings are at Fajr time, and good for me as you can help me unwind during my mini-holiday here.'

My jaw dropped.

Aunt Amel pulled an orange texta with no lid from the front pocket of her fluffy nightrobe.

'What time do you think is suitable to start the day? Three a.m.? Four?'

She looked around at each of us, hoping for some

feedback. She held the texta to the scribbly paper, like she was interviewing us, poised for an answer.

'We don't wake up that early,' Kholoud said, her voice sharp.

'Very well – five a.m!'

Aunt Amel jotted this onto her paper. There was no time to react before she moved on.

'I have determined seven tasks to make this holiday most pleasant. One for each of you.'

She walked over to Omar, who still had his eyes closed and looked a bit like Mr Kostiki the other night. His body swayed in a weird, gentle way. I wondered how people could possibly sleep standing up. Aunt Amel didn't seem to notice, though. She pointed her finger at him as she held the paper too close to her eyes and began to read.

'Task one. Omar, you are on your L-plates. You will drive me everywhere I need to go. This helps you because I can teach you everything about driving and you can add it to your logbook. And – bonus – I get my own personal chauffeur!' Aunt Amel grinned.

She took a step sideways to face Kholoud, who had her arms folded and looked like she was chewing something.

'Task two. My dear, you have a fine eye for beauty and fashion. I would love to hire you as my personal stylist and beauty expert.'

My big sister beamed. Kholoud loves make-up and clothes more than anyone. I could tell from the look on her face that it was like a dream job she hadn't even applied for. But she tried to stay cool.

'Okay, sure. I don't mind helping you out. I have some samples in my room I can try on you later.'

Aunt Amel clapped her hands together and then spun in a circle. She lost her footing for a moment and stumbled, but managed to stay upright. Then she turned to the twins.

'Suha and Layla. Two wise souls.' She paused to squint at them in an *oh, so cute* way, then went back to her list. 'Your dad says you make the best tea in all the western suburbs. I've drunk your tea, and I agree! This task is perfect, because I drink tea by the gallon. You will be my personal tea- and cookie-makers. Well, you will be my little assistants, really – get me whatever I need, whenever I need it, including tea and cookies.'

The twins frowned. They turned to each other then turned back to Aunt Amel. Suha cleared her throat.

'Excuse me, Aunt Amel. This isn't reasonable. We enjoy making tea, but we shouldn't be forced to do anything we don't want to do.'

'Oh no, no, no. You misunderstood me, my girls.' Aunt Amel leaned her long body over, bringing her face closer to my sisters'. 'What you need to do is refine your baking and tea-making skills, because I feel you could certainly win awards.'

'Awards?' my sisters stuttered at the same time.

'Yes – worldwide recognition. I can see you on that famous cooking show. You know, the one with the funny aprons…'

Aunt Amel was waving her arms around, staring into the air, and my sisters weren't frowning anymore – they were glowing. So Aunt Amel flicked her head towards me and Huda.

'Akeal, ah, little Akoolie! We need a very important person to keep things clean around here. You will be, let's agree, the butler of the house.'

My mind raced. I thought a butler carried a tray and wore a black vest. Most of the ones I'd seen on TV had no hair. They were all my dad's age, with posh accents.

A million questions exploded in my head, but she just kept going.

'Hoodie Boodie! You're a bit like Akeal, I suppose. Very, uhh…useful. You will help Akeal. He'll the butler of the house and you will be the maid.'

'A maid? A maid for who?' My sister scratched and shook her head at the same time.

'For m— For the family. Your job is very important because you keep everything tidy and running flawlessly.'

'I don't know what *flawlessly* means,' Huda shot back.

'Hudie, it means your very important job is to keep us all happy, all the time! Make it a game, if you'd like!'

Aunt Amel pulled a tissue out of the tissue box on the kitchen bench and popped it onto Huda's head.

'You see, just like a real maid!'

Before Huda had a chance to protest or complain, Aunt Amel read out one last task: 'And Raheed's job is to stay with me all day. We're going to spend my holiday together.'

I realised my baby brother wasn't in the room with us, but figured he was still asleep.

As if she'd read my mind, Aunt Amel repeated: 'All day and all night. With me. My holiday buddy. He'll stay by my side until I'm relaxed and rested enough, knowing you're all doing your little jobs perfectly.' And Aunt Amel winked.

I had seen Aunt Amel hold Raheed. He always tried to climb back over to Mum.

Aunt Amel dug deep into her robe pocket again and pulled out more bits of messily scrunched-up paper, each with one of our names on them. She tossed them at us.

'I understand you are small, and children do forget things. So here is your list of things to do, just in case.' The way she said it made it sound like she was doing us a favour.

Dad's alarm clock suddenly went off, interrupting our thoughts as we picked our lists up off the floor. A man's voice reciting the call to prayer in Arabic blared from the small silver mosque-shaped clock that sat on the kitchen shelf. Dad had set the alarm to go off for each prayer, and it was time for the first of the day.

I thought Aunt Amel might remember then that Muslims don't make kids act like small helpers and cleaners. I thought she might realise her paper lists were unfair, especially since the man's voice was reminding her to pray instead.

Aunt Amel flinched. Then she walked slowly over to the clock and gazed at it for a moment before grabbing it and bolting towards the fridge. She opened the freezer door and shoved it in, the athan sound disappearing abruptly as she slammed the freezer door shut.

My eyes darted around at each of my siblings.

Kholoud's face was still; she wasn't even blinking. She lifted her hand and put it over her mouth. Even she knew this was going too far.

Omar's eyes had shot open when the athan went off. He stared at the freezer door and then at Aunt Amel. Then he stepped forward. I noticed the list of chores Aunt Amel had chucked at him was caught in the collar of his pyjama shirt.

'You can't do that,' Omar said. 'That belongs to our dad, and it reminds us to pray on time.' He sounded brave.

The wrinkles around Aunt Amel's eyes creased and she pressed her lips together.

'Omie, don't fret. I'm just a little sensitive to noise. So remember to be super quiet as you all go about your tasks.'

She glanced at the scrunched-up paper stuck in Omar's shirt and took one step closer to him. He was almost as tall as her, but she patted him on the head.

'Not to worry, the clock is safe, tucked away until your parents get back. Just focus on your lists, so we can all have a comfortable and happy two weeks.'

She clicked her fingers again as Omar opened his mouth to speak.

'Now, let's start the day! On to your tasks!' She jabbed a finger at the twins. 'You two. Tea. My room. Five minutes. Bring cookies in forty-five minutes. With more tea.'

In the kitchen doorway, she stopped one last time.

'Please, children. We all want to keep Raheed happy while I'm here, don't we?'

And with that, she was gone.

Huda gulped loudly. For a moment, we all just stood there staring at each other. Huda opened her mouth to say something, but Kholoud put a painted fingernail to Huda's lips.

'She has Raheed. Just get on with it, Huda. It's no big deal – just do what she said.'

'Yeah, Huda, we have cookies to practise making...' Layla chimed in.

'...so we can be famous!' Suha finished for her. She looked like she'd just had too much red cordial. She was already pulling a rolling pin from the drawer.

'But...' said Huda.

I looked at the paper Aunt Amel had thrown at me, then glanced around at the others'. My and Huda's lists were three times as long as everyone else's.

My first chore was to scoop up the chicken poo in the backyard and put it in a big poo pile. I wasn't convinced that butlers scooped poo. I couldn't imagine them doing it in their nice shirts. Huda's first chore was to scrub the toilets – and after that, to change all the bedsheets.

I pulled on my gumboots, chucked on my raincoat and went to find my head-torch. It was freezing outside, and the sun was barely up. Then again, maybe Aunt Amel was right – maybe all the blessings of the day were in the morning.

I passed Huda in the bathroom doorway as I headed outside, and we locked eyes. She stood there in the dim light holding the toilet brush in her hand. Her bottom lip quivered. She was about to cry.

I wanted to tell her she would be okay. I wanted to say that she didn't need to scrub the toilets, or do the beds. But I also knew a little hard work was a good thing – Dad always tells me that. It was only for a little while. Until Mum and Dad were back. Until we knew Raheed could join the rest of us again.

So, instead, I only looked at my sister and hoped she knew what I was thinking before I slipped outside into the cold.

Michael

This place doesn't look or feel like an airport. Amira leads us past palm trees and water fountains, and seemingly endless fancy shops selling jewellery, make-up and Arabian-looking souvenirs. There are huge blue signs everywhere, in both Arabic and English. I test out my Arabic reading skills, but they must've left out some important grammar because none of it makes sense to me. I'm unsure if it's brighter in here or outside in the hot sun – the shiny tiles and silver and gold things everywhere make me squint.

The men in this airport walk around in white abayas, like the ones I've seen Dad's friends wear at the mosque. They look like they've spent five hours in front of a mirror with a small pair of scissors, making sure each little hair on their beard and goatee is perfect. I've never seen men look so cool or so clean. I know if I ever wear a white abaya dress, I'll have spaghetti-sauce stains on it before dinner is finished.

The women wear hijabs, but pin them differently to how I've seen it done in Australia – almost like they've flicked the hijab over their hair and it's landed perfectly, like fabric over a beehive. I think that they must have the darkest eyes and the longest eyelashes in the world. Most of them are dressed in black, which is draped right down to their toes, but their huge gold bangles pop out of their sleeves and make them sparkle.

Amira walks us through some security checks, then past more glossy fashion stores and some cafés. Huda slows and elbows me.

'Oi, what's this all about? This is meant to be our holiday stopover. Where is she taking us?' she whispers.

'I dunno, but Martin said we have to stay with her.' I keep my eyes on Amira, worried she might turn around and catch us talking about her.

'Let's make a run for it.'

My eyes almost pop out of my eye sockets. 'Make a run for it? Are you crazy?'

'Yeh, let's ditch her and go have some fun. Look at all the food and fun we're missing out on. Check out all those cool shops with the little teacups and other fancy things!' Huda flaps her hands around in every direction, like I haven't noticed where we are.

'Huda, no way!' I hiss. 'Amira seems nice, and besides, if we run away we'll be caught and sent back to Melbourne. That's if we even manage to find the boarding gate for our next flight.'

Amira stops suddenly, and we almost walk into her. 'How about a spot of shopping, kids? And then some dinner?'

My sister misses a beat, so I nudge her and she speaks up. 'Um, sure, Miss Amira. Why not?'

Amira leads us into one of the shiny gift stores and waits patiently as we wander the polished aisles. I pick a small golden camel with a shiny red blanket on its back. Huda finally decides on a green lantern, and I pay with a hundred-dollar note I've surreptitiously pulled from the bottom of my bag.

'You never know, brother, a genie might pop out and give us three wishes,' Huda giggles.

I don't have the heart to tell her it isn't a lamp.

Amira beams when we show her our souvenirs. She fiddles with the red blanket on my camel, lifting a tiny latch, and it pops open like the boot of a car. I can't wait to put something secret in it, like Tic Tacs.

'Who wants dinner?' Amira asks us.

'Yes, please,' I say as I tuck my camel into the front compartment of my bag.

Huda grabs her tummy and squeezes it with both hands. 'I'm starving!'

I notice a toilet sign nearby and check my watch. I'm unsure how I'm meant to work out when to pray, with all the time differences and changing of countries, but Dad always tells me it's about having the right intention.

'Amira, do you mind if I use the bathroom for a minute, please?'

'Sure!' She walks us over to the entrance. 'I'll be waiting right here with your sister. Call out if you need anything.'

I walk through the grey door, hoping there'll be no one inside so I can do my wudu – and that there'll be enough room to lift my foot into the sink. That's always the worst bit about doing wudu in a public place. That, or someone walking in on you and wondering what the heck you're doing washing your feet in a sink.

There are five cubicles and they're all empty. The place is clean and smells like air freshener. Pretty good for a public toilet. I roll my sleeves up to my elbows and turn on the tap. The water's freezing cold.

I quickly wash my hands and rinse out my mouth. Then I splash water in my nose, on my face, and on my arms, three times. I wet my palms and run them across the top of my head so that my hair gets all damp. The iciness of the water gives me a chill but makes me feel fresh at the same time. Like I'm rinsing all the bad stuff away. Like Aunt Amel is disappearing down the drain, along with all the water dripping off me.

The tap stops running automatically, and I bend to untie my shoelaces then slip my right foot out of my shoe. I hop around on my other foot as I take off my smelly, three-day-old sock with wet hands. There's nowhere to put it without getting it dirty or drenched, so I hold it between my front teeth. The pong is revolting.

I lift my right foot and cram it into the sink, hit the tap again, and let the water run between each of my toes. I'm rotating my foot around a bit, to make sure water gets all the way up to my ankle, when I hear chatter outside and the grey door into the bathroom swings open. The shock of being sprung makes me lose my balance, but my foot gets caught in the sink, stopping me from falling backwards. A boy about my age is standing in the doorway staring at me. I spit the sock into my hand.

'Ummm...sorry,' he mutters.

We both stand there frozen for a moment.

'Are you okay?' he asks. He's frowning, but not in an angry way – more like he feels sorry for me. His eyes look like little blue triangles in the reflected bathroom light.

'I'm fine!' I try dislodging my foot from the sink, but my hand slips on the wet sink in the process and I fall back onto the floor. I laugh to try and look like I'm cool – even though I am clearly not.

The boy stretches out his arm to help me. He's wearing the same grey T-shirt that Omar bought from the surf shop at home a couple of weeks ago. I realise that he speaks like me – with an Australian accent. It's not what I'd expected, here in Dubai.

'Thanks,' I say, taking his arm and pulling myself up. He doesn't seem like he's going to leave, so I pull my sock on and try to slip my foot back into my runner. I'm still dripping and I fumble.

The boy glances down at my shoes. 'Oh, wicked, you have those awesome new basketball sneakers!'

'Um…yeh…my dad got them for me at the end of last term,' I say as I finally get my runner back onto my foot.

'I've been begging my parents for them for ages, but they won't budge. Do they really help you jump higher?' he asks.

I'm a bit embarrassed that this conversation is taking place in the toilets, but also relieved he's noticed something other than me hanging off the sink with a sock in my mouth

'Not really,' I say. 'They're pretty comfy, though, and they look cool.' I chuckle.

The boy smiles. We both know that these are the coolest runners ever, or at least this season. 'I'm joining a new basketball team next month,' he says.

'I'm on a team too. Where are you from?' I ask as I wipe my face with a paper towel. My brain is starting to work again now that I feel a little less wet and my shoes are back on.

'I've moved to a new suburb in Melbourne. I think the team's called the Williamstown Warriors,' he says.

My mouth drops open. 'No *way*! That's my team!'

I can't believe it. We're probably living around the corner from each other.

The boy grins. 'Whoa! I'm Michael, by the way.' He sticks out his arm again, and this time we shake hands.

'I'm Akeal.'

'Huh?'

'Akeal.'

Michael says my name to himself twice, like he's prac-tising how to say it. 'So, why didn't you have your shoe on?' he asks. 'And how come you were all wet?'

I consider telling him that I spilled juice on myself, but I know it's haram to lie. 'I was…um…I was making wudu.'

I can see he doesn't know what that means from the way he stares at me blankly. 'Wud-what?'

But before I can answer, he jumps in again: 'Is it true they're changing the team uniform to black and red?

I haven't been able to get it yet, because they said new ones might be coming out.'

I haven't heard that rumour, but I'm glad he's changed the subject himself. 'Um, I dunno, to be honest. But black and red would be so cool.'

Michael grins and shifts his feet. 'Hey, I'm busting.' He darts to the closest cubicle and slams the door shut.

I'm not sure whether to wait for him or not. I remember that Amira is waiting. 'Michael, I'd better head off. I'll catch you back in Melbourne, okay!'

'No worries, man! See ya soon!'

I hear Michael pull down a bunch of toilet paper and figure he might need a bit of privacy anyway.

No Escape

I watched the second hand move slowly around the clock above the whiteboard in my classroom. My eyelids felt like they were made of clay.

'So, what's the answer, Akeal?' Mr Morrison was pointing to a division question on the board, and I realised the whole class was staring at me.

I swallowed hard and wiped some drool off my lip. 'Umm...sixty-four?'

'Please try to stay awake in class. The answer is eight.'

Mr Morrison rambled some more – something about our projects being due – and then he said the words I was dying to hear.

'Pack-up time!'

I shoved my homework and pencil case into my bag. I knew I had to be quick – Aunt Amel was waiting. I quite like walking home, but Aunt Amel had insisted she and Omar pick us up after school. 'To save time,' she'd said.

'Excuse me, Akeal. Can I see you for a minute?' Mr Morrison called.

My heart plopped into my guts and I dragged my feet over to his desk.

The first early morning was easy. Waking up at Fajr time isn't new to me. Sometimes Dad and I pray and then go on early-morning fishing trips. But I don't usually have to stay awake dusting and scrubbing until midnight. It was only day two with Aunt Amel, and I was already exhausted.

'Sure, Mr Morrison. Is anything wrong?'

Mr Morrison was wearing his burgundy woollen vest with the five big buttons. The bottom one fell off earlier in the year, but I don't think he noticed. Or maybe he doesn't care. Someone had already turned out the light, so his beard looked almost black. Usually it's more golden-brown, with a few bits of grey. He waited for the last of the kids to leave the room.

'I've been a bit worried about you this week.'

I didn't say anything.

'Is there something going on that you want to tell me about?'

I looked out the window. Anything to not have to look at him.

'C'mon, buddy. Tell me what's going on. You haven't been your usual self. You've been half asleep. Your spelling test this morning...I couldn't even make out some of the words...'

Mr Morrison seemed like he really cared. I took a breath. 'You know how Mum and Dad have gone overseas?' I started.

He nodded.

'Our babysitter, you know, she expects us to do a lot of stuff.'

'Like chores?' Mr Morrison blinked his small almond eyes, twice. He's a blinker.

'Yeh. Like, she makes us do different jobs before school and after school.'

Mr Morrison crossed his arms. 'Well, that's about taking responsibility, buddy. You have a big family, so everyone has to pull their weight. Would it be fair if she had to do everything for you?'

'No, but—'

'Would it be right if you left everything up to your older brothers and sisters?'

'No, of course—'

'Good. You get it. What you need to do is have a bit of a think about time management. When I was your age,

65

I made sure I did all my chores first thing – none of that jumping on the TV for four hours – and then I got onto my homework.'

'But she makes us get up so early to—'

'Early bird gets the worm!' Mr Morrison chuckled and shook his head.

My shoulders slumped. I realised there was no point. 'Yeh, you're right. Thanks, Mr Morrison.'

I turned to leave. I could picture Aunt Amel in the carpark right now, leaning over Omar and beeping the horn in front of all the other kids.

'Good lad. Remember – time management!' he said as I walked out of the room.

Huda was waiting for me outside the classroom door. The dark rings around her eyes were worse than mine.

'What was all that about?' she puffed as she tried to keep up with me.

'Nothing. I tried to talk to him, but he didn't listen.'

'Crap. I thought Mr Morrison would help. We need to hurry – I saw her from my classroom window beeping the horn and throwing lollies at kids. She's going to embarrass us, especially if she's waving her hijab around like a flag again.'

Luckily, by the time we reached my parents' car most of the schoolkids had already left. But a few were still hanging around, picking up lollies off the ground. We quickly jumped into the back seat.

'The besties are here!' Aunt Amel cooed from the front passenger seat. She twisted around to face us. 'And how was your day today, children?'

'Good,' me and Huda said at the same time. Then we both stared out the window.

Omar glanced at me in the rear-view mirror as he turned on the ignition. In the last two days, I was sure he'd driven Aunt Amel about the distance between Melbourne and Perth. Three times over. He'd taken her to all her coffee dates and lunches, and waited for her at the cinemas. The worst, he'd said, was when he had to watch her from outside restaurants while she had dinner with people who she called 'suitors'.

She took Raheed *everywhere* with her, too – except for when she took me and Huda to or from school. Then she left him with the twins. I hadn't seen him since the night Mum and Dad left.

'So, what did we learn at school?' she pushed. She was still twisted around, staring at us.

'Nothing,' I said.

Huda shrugged her shoulders.

Aunt Amel pressed her lips together and then swung back to face the front. But she wasn't done with the conversation.

'The twins have been working hard to perfect their biscotti,' she blathered. 'I must say, their custard-cream biscuits are my favourite so far – with a nice mug of oolong tea.'

The drive home was short. I wished she'd just let us walk.

'*And* I had the best pedi and mani today. Look at my nails! First I told Kholoud I wanted red, but then I changed my mind. Aren't they divine?'

She lifted her hands to show us. They were a metallic bronze. Worse than red.

When we pulled into our driveway, my sister lunged out of the car before Omar had even pulled the handbrake. I followed suit, but Aunt Amel was faster. She leapt between us and the front door and grinned.

'Wait, children! Come, come, my little butler and maid. Remind me, what is your evening routine?'

Aunt Amel already knew the answer. She'd asked us this very same question yesterday afternoon.

Huda just sighed, so I decided to answer for the both of us.

'Put all our school uniforms in the wash, hang them out, put fresh sheets on the beds, do the dishes, vacuum the rooms and...'

This was the bit I hated the most. Aunt Amel peered down at me. I knew she was excited. 'And...?'

'Give you a foot rub and scalp massage before tidying the bathroom.'

Aunt Amel patted me on the head. 'Good boy!' She turned to Huda and said pointedly, 'Remember, it takes a village! Your parents would be so proud of you! Now, off you go, the night is still young! But keep it down – we don't want to wake Raheed from his afternoon nap!'

We raced to get away from her, though I spared a thought for my big brother Omar and looked back to see him still sitting in the car, slumped over the steering wheel.

In the kitchen, the smell of baked goodies filled my nose. Hundreds of different biscuits, muffins and cupcakes lined the benches. For a second, I thought I was in the wrong house. But then I saw Suha slouched over the counter, surrounded by muffin tins and baking trays.

'*How* did you manage to make all of this after school?' Huda asked, licking her lips.

'We didn't,' Suha mumbled.

'You didn't bake this?'

A second voice chimed in: 'We didn't go to school.' It was Layla. She was on the ground – I could see her feet poking out from behind the counter.

'You stayed home to bake?' I asked.

'Yeh. We haven't been to school all week.'

I'd assumed Omar and Aunt Amel had been dropping them off every morning after us. Huda shivered and snorted at the same time. Suha's eyes welled with tears.

'We've been trying so hard to make the best recipes,' she said. 'Aunt Amel says we're getting better but we're not there yet. Not good enough to be on TV.'

I picked up a mini cupcake with fancy red icing on top that looked like a rose and shoved it into my mouth. Huda did the same.

'Tastes pretty good to me!' I said between chews.

I wanted to stay and breathe in the sugary smells and make my sisters feel better, but I heard Aunt Amel's footsteps on the verandah. 'C'mon, Huda, she's coming.'

Huda swiped a chocolate cookie, then both of us grabbed two more cupcakes and we headed to our rooms to change into our cleaning clothes.

Grabbing the empty washing basket from the laundry, I couldn't help but think of all the bowls with dried batter and crusty pans we'd have to scrub tonight. There was no point collecting the twins' uniforms for washing – I wished I'd known that yesterday. So I headed to Kholoud's room, knocking gently on my big sister's door.

Nothing. I knocked a little harder. Then I heard it – a muffled sob.

I pushed open her bedroom door just enough to poke my head through. 'Kholoud...you okay?'

She was sitting on her bed, but she wasn't alone. She was leaning on Huda's shoulder, and Huda was stroking our big sister's head.

Huda looked at me with sad eyes then turned back to Kholoud. 'Sshhhh, it's okay. You're going to be an amazing make-up artist one day.'

Kholoud bawled. The top part of Huda's cleaning shirt was covered in blobs of tears and snot now, as well as its bleach marks and some gross-looking stains.

'If it makes you feel any better,' Huda went on, 'I love the way you do my make-up, and the way you give me advice about colour-matching.'

Kholoud lifted her head and looked at Huda. I thought she was going to say something, but instead she pulled a tissue out of her pocket and blew her nose. I let myself into the room and closed the door behind me.

Kholoud turned to me. 'I really do my best. I lay out her clothes every morning, even her accessories and shoes – just like she tells me. I do her hair, and that's the worst, because she barely has any. But she always complains. She says I'm trying to make her into someone she's not, and then she makes me start over.'

I didn't understand this making-yourself-beautiful stuff, but I understood how it felt when your best wasn't good enough. I gave my big sister a hug.

Just then the door creaked open and the twins staggered in. They plonked themselves onto the bed. I was surprised Kholoud let them do that – she rarely lets any of us in her room, unless we have secrets or bubblegum to share. Omar must've seen the twins, because he followed a moment later and closed the door behind him.

'Where is she?' Huda asked.

Layla stuffed her face into the doona.

'She's outside talking to Mr Kostiki,' said Omar.

Perhaps I was imagining it, but he looked scrawnier than he had a few days ago. His eyes were red and he rubbed at them.

'She just finished lecturing me on how to drive in a dust storm. We've never had a dust storm – let alone had to drive in one! I don't know what planet she's on!'

We nodded in agreement. Layla removed her face from the doona so she could speak. 'I can't bake anymore. My hands are about to fall off. She doesn't even drink half the cups of tea we bring her. I'm falling behind at school, and I think we've used up all the flour in the supermarket.'

We all looked at each other.

'What are we gonna do?' Huda asked.

No one spoke at first, because none of us knew the answer. But then I realised it was simple.

'We tell Mum and Dad!'

'How do we do that? If they ring she'll just tell them we're out, or asleep. She won't want us talking to them. And we can't call them – she hides the phone. I've looked everywhere for it.' Kholoud had clearly thought about this already. Mum and Dad don't believe kids should have phones, so there was only one in the house. And Aunt Amel had it.

'I'll tell Mr Kostiki then,' Huda chimed in.

'She doesn't let you go over there anymore,' I reminded my sister.

'Leave it to me, folks. Leave it to me.'

☁

It was eleven p.m. and Huda and I still hadn't finished our butler and maid duties, but Aunt Amel wanted her massage.

'Hud Hud, Akoolie, I'm reaaady!'

Aunt Amel was already laid out on Dad's recliner couch. She ripped off her hijab. I heard Huda whimper beside me, but she stepped forward and took her spot near Aunt Amel's head.

'Make sure your hands are warm this time,' Aunt Amel snapped. 'Last time you gave my head a chill with your bitterly cold fingers.' And she closed her eyes and rested her head back.

Huda breathed into her hands and then rubbed them together. She looked at me and shrugged her shoulders, then glanced towards Aunt Amel's feet with big eyes as if to say, *Your job is way worse.*

'Akeal, where are you? Hurry up, please – I need to relax! My feeties are waiting.'

Aunt Amel wriggled her long toes. Thank God she was wearing socks. One was blue with stripes, and the other was green with dots, but I'd rather odd socks than no socks at all. I stepped forward and rubbed my hands together like Huda, to buy myself some time.

'Come on, children, I'm tired! Shopping all day has made me sore!'

I kneeled beside Aunt Amel, then I reached in and began to knead the balls of her feet. Huda closed her eyes and did the same on Aunt Amel's head. I could tell my sister was trying to imagine she was somewhere else.

'Too hard, Huda. I want to unwind, not have my scalp squashed!' Aunt Amel grumbled.

Huda pulled a face and poked her tongue out at Aunt Amel, who still had her eyes closed.

I muffled my laugh with a cough and moved my hands towards Aunt Amel's toes. This was the worst bit – massaging toes. They felt like talons on a bird's foot. I squeezed each one quickly then ran my hands down to her heels, hoping for it all to be over.

It only took a minute for Aunt Amel's breathing to turn into a long, drawn-out snore. That was when Huda and I pulled away and raced to the bathroom as fast as we could. We both squeezed a tonne of soap into our palms and scrubbed our hands ferociously with hot water, not caring if it burned us.

Huda flicked the water from her fingers and sighed. 'Might as well finish wiping the bathroom down since we're here,' she said, pulling the disinfectant spray and cloth from the cupboard below the sink. She sprayed the shower screen and began to wipe it clean. We'd already scrubbed the bathroom this morning, but Aunt Amel always inspected our work, and it was never good enough – no matter what the job.

I can see streak marks on the mirror.

I can still see dust.

You haven't rolled the socks into a ball properly.

You need to organise all the cups in order of colour and size.

I didn't get it. Aunt Amel was a grub. Her scarves were always ripped and discoloured. Her clothes had stains on them. She wore odd socks. She always missed when she threw something in the bin, and never bothered to pick it up.

Huda finished wiping over the shower screen while I replaced the empty toilet roll.

'Right. I'm going to tell him now.'

My sister dropped the spray and hopped onto the lid of the toilet. She yanked open the small bathroom window. Huda's small, but I wasn't sure she was *that* small. I was even less sure whether it was a good idea to go to Mr Kostiki's house in the middle of the night.

'He might be asleep,' I said nervously. 'Just try tomorrow.'

'You know she doesn't let us out of her sight. It's now or never. Cover for me.'

My sister hoisted herself up to the tiny window and managed to slither through. I heard her fall onto the ground below with an *oomph*, then scramble across the front yard.

I jumped onto the toilet seat to see whether she'd reached Mr Kostiki's house just in time to glimpse her shoeless feet dash past his letterbox. A moment later, there was banging on Mr Kostiki's front door. Nothing. She banged again, then I heard talking: Huda's high-pitched voice and Mr Kostiki's accent. I couldn't make out the words, so I pushed my head up closer to the open window.

'Birdwatching at night, are we, Akoolie?' came Aunt Amel's voice, right in my ear. I almost fell off the toilet seat in shock. 'And what have you seen, hmmm?'

Aunt Amel poked her head out the window. She was tall enough to do that easily. I knew Huda was a goner. And sure enough, a split-second later Aunt Amel flicked her body around and raced out of the bathroom. I heard the front door open and then slam shut. I hopped back onto the toilet and watched her lope across the lawn and over to Mr Kostiki's house. Moments later, Aunt Amel was leading Huda back home.

The Incident

I rejoin Amira and my sister outside the bathroom.

'Ugh, your head is all wet. You look slimy.' Huda never feels she has to hide her thoughts from me.

I wipe the top of my head and flick away the remaining beads of water.

Amira leads us further through the airport until we reach some huge sliding doors with cartoon pictures printed across them. At the top is a sign in Arabic, then English. I don't bother trying to read the Arabic this time. *Unaccompanied Minors Lounge.*

Amira swipes a card dangling from her hip over a sensor-pad and the doors slip open. The room bursts with colour. On one side are some funky red kids' couches, plus a couple of round blue tables covered with fresh paper and brand-new textas. On the other side, a giant screen faces a smattering of lounge chairs. Stacked up beside the screen are video-game controllers, tablets, board games and books. This must be Jannah on Earth for kids.

Amira asks whether we'd like lasagne or beef burgers for dinner. I say I want a burger. Huda says she wants six.

'Let's start with one and see how you go,' Amira says and heads into a small kitchen area to get our food.

My sister chucks her backpack on the floor and plonks herself down at one of the blue tables. She starts to colour in one of the clean sheets of paper. I want to throw myself onto one of the lounge chairs, but I know I need to pray before anything else.

I unzip my backpack and pull out the compass keychain Dad gave me two years ago on Eid. I always keep it with me, even when I'm at school. The little red arrow points to a little black Kaaba, telling me which direction to face. Holding it in my hands makes me feel close to Dad again, and I feel tears prickle my eyes, but they're not bad tears – they're tears that remind me how much I love my baba.

The green, fluffy carpet looks freshly vacuumed, so I lift my hands to pray, just as Amira brings out three huge, cheesy burgers – one for each of us. My tummy rumbles as I place my forehead on the soft floor. By the time I'm finished, my eyes are dry.

Amira drops us to the departure gate, just in time for our departure to Beirut. Miss Rosetta is standing at the doorway leading to the plane with her arms crossed. Huda grunts when she sees her. Amira passes Miss Rosetta our passports and the new tickets for this flight. Miss Rosetta pretends to smile – I can tell because her eyes don't look as happy as the rest of her face. Amira is so caring. I don't think I'll ever forget her sparkly green eyes and the way everything about her felt cheery and safe.

Huda tugs at Amira's sleeve and borrows a fancy black pen, then fumbles around in her backpack for something to write on. She pulls out an old piece of crumpled paper with orange writing scrawled across it – Aunt Amel's list of jobs. My sister looks at it in her palm, and then at me. Then she does her best to unwrinkle it, and scribbles her school email address across the orange scrawl.

'I'd love to be friends with you,' my sister says to Amira as she passes her the pen and the half-scrunched bit of paper. She picks nervously at a cuticle. Her little round face has gone almost the same red as Raheed's rosy cheeks.

Amira gives Huda a smile, bigger than all the others we've seen so far. 'I'd love to be friends with you too, Huda.'

Huda throws her arms around Amira's waist. I glance around and realise we're holding up the queue. People want to get on the plane, not wait for a couple of kids to say their final goodbyes to their customer service agent.

Miss Rosetta taps her heel on the tiles, then taps my sister on the shoulder. 'Time to hop on the plane now, children.'

Huda lets go of Amira, gives her one last wave, and then squints up at Miss Rosetta. 'Where's Martin?'

Miss Rosetta raises one eyebrow. Then she purses her lips and jabs her finger towards the plane.

My sister nods once and skips ahead. I grab our passports and tickets from Miss Rosetta and follow behind.

We meet Martin at the entrance of the plane.

'Hooda and Akeaw! Lovely to see you again. I trust Amira took good care of you and showed you the best of Dubai Airport.' He checks the tickets for our seat numbers.

'She was great!' trills Huda. 'We almost became best friends forever, but we had to leave.'

Martin raises his eyebrows, as though he's impressed.

'Akeaw, was Dubai Airport everything you thought it would be?' I like that Martin asks me this. Huda hogs all the attention whenever she can.

'I loved it,' I say. 'One day, when this is all over—' Huda shoots me a warning look, and I choke a little. 'I mean... what I meant was... when I'm a bit older... I'll come back.'

'That's excellent. Good to hear!' He hands us back our tickets. 'You'll be in row number fifty-six, seats *A* and *B*. And, lucky you, you'll have a spare seat next to you today.'

'Thank you, Martin,' me and Huda say at the same time.

Martin gestures to show us which aisle to walk down and points out what side our seats are on. 'I'll be down to check on you in a little while.'

This plane is almost twice the size of the one we flew on from Melbourne. There are three seats on each side of the aircraft, by the windows, and four in the middle. They stretch on for what looks like hundreds of rows.

We're the first on the plane, and we take our time getting into our spots. Huda takes the seat closest to the window again. I sit next to her, and we keep the third seat for our stuff.

The plane fills up quickly, and before we know it they play the safety video. After that, we're in the air. Martin pops past and I give him a thumbs up. Everything is going perfectly.

I decide to chill out with a movie and begin to flick through the options on the screen in front of me. There are a million to choose from, and I read each summary, finally deciding on a new-release movie about aliens and zombies that Mum and Dad would *never* let me watch at home.

Just as I'm about to hit *play*, Huda elbows me. 'Gotta go to the dunny. Move over.'

She squeezes past me before I can even lift my tray-table, tangling my headphones. I grab my headset before she drags it down the aisle, pop it back over my ears, and hit *play* again on my movie. An alien begins to attack a family of zombies, and I sigh happily.

Just as the zombies are about to rip off the alien's head, through the gap between the seats ahead, I spot Huda charging back up the plane aisle. Her hijab is twisted to the side, and tears stream down her face.

I hit *pause* on the movie, right at the bit where blood spurts out of the alien's ears. Huda's in such a hurry to get back to her seat that she's bumping into people and knocking things off their tray-tables. She squeezes past me and curls into a ball on her seat.

'Huda, what's wrong? What happened?'

She doesn't answer. I wonder if she finally saw her reflection properly in the toilet mirror and realised she looks a bit too dressed up.

'If it's about what you're wearing, don't worry, you look okay.' I've heard it's okay to tell a white lie to make people feel better.

She sobs harder and covers her face with her hands.

'You look all right. Really.'

Huda whispers, 'Are you sure, Akeal?'

'Of course I'm sure. Would I lie to you?'

I'm about to hit *play* to see whether the zombies will actually eat the leftover alien bits when Huda speaks again.

'Because the boy called me a little terrorist. He told me to take "that thing" off my head.'

I feel like I've been hit by a cricket bat. I wonder if I heard her wrong.

'What are you talking about?' I stutter the words. They stick in my throat.

She sits up and wipes her wet cheeks with the sleeve of her jumper. Then she sniffs and rubs her nose with her fist.

'I went to the fancy toilets at the front of the plane. The ones for the rich people. I was waiting my turn to go in and an older boy came and stood next to me. He was looking at me a lot. Like he was gonna say I look nice in my scarf or something.'

My sister's voice is croaky and soft, and I can barely make out some of the words she's saying. She pauses and swallows. Hard. Like it hurts to talk.

'Then he said Muslims are bad, and that I probably want to hurt him. I don't understand what he was talking about. I don't even have a toy gun. And then...'

Huda's breathing gets deeper and heavier. She can't get the words out through her tears.

'And then what happened, Huda?' I need to know, but I don't want to hear it.

'Then he grabbed my hijab and tried to pull it off.' Huda's tears take over and she curls up again.

Her face is red and wet. Her fringe sticks out of the front of her scarf and a few diamantes are falling off. I put my arm over her, so she's wrapped up like she's in a cocoon.

Martin dashes towards us from the front end of the plane and kneels down. His face is flushed, and his voice is serious.

'I'm sorry about what just happened, Hooda.'

Huda doesn't look at Martin.

'Sometimes people can be...' Martin pauses. He doesn't know the word he's looking for.

'Mean,' says Huda quietly, from inside her cocoon.

'Racist,' I say. I've heard of stuff like this, and worse, happening on the news.

Martin nods. 'But I don't want you to worry. The boy won't be coming anywhere near you for the rest of the flight.'

Huda slowly unravels herself from her ball. She blinks her eyes a few times and clears her throat. Then she wipes her runny nose with the sleeve of her jumper again.

'It's okay, Martin. That boy is nasty, but I feel sorry for him for being so stupid,' she says through sniffles.

Martin takes a clean tissue from his pocket and hands it to my sister, but she waves her hand to say she doesn't need it. She wipes her nose with her sleeve again instead.

'I know it probably doesn't mean much right now, but I think you look lovely in your scarf, Hooda,' says Martin.

Huda half-smiles. 'You think so, Martin?'

She's still sniffling, but I know she's hoping he keeps going with the compliments.

'Yes, pink is totally your colour.' Martin's normal voice is back. He leans over and adjusts her hijab so it's sitting right again on her head. Huda closes her eyes while he does it, as though she's at the hairdresser.

Martin knows just what it takes to make her feel better. I feel a bit awkward sitting there between the two of them, but I'm glad my sister isn't crying anymore.

'How about an ice-cream?' says Martin, rubbing his hands together.

Huda's eyes widen. 'Yes, please! Can my brother have one too?'

Huda. No matter what happens, she still thinks of me.

'Okay, ice-cream first, and then spaghetti and meat-balls.' Martin grins and heads off again down the aisle.

There's silence between me and my sister. I don't know whether she wants to talk about it. I don't know what to say.

She speaks first.

'Don't worry about it, Akeal. He was just a dumb kid.'

'Yeh, he is dumb. Don't be upset, Buds.' I only call her Buds when she's feeling sad or when she's done something really cool, like got an *A* in sports class.

My sister nods and sniffs. 'He was mean. But it made me feel better that he was wearing those ugly white runners Mum was gonna get you before Dad bought you these cool ones.' Huda points down to my feet.

Something clicks in my brain. The question comes like an itch that I need to scratch. 'What did this kid look like, anyway?' I try to sound casual.

My sister thinks for a moment. 'He had big blue eyes, brown hair – shorter than yours. He was wearing a grey T-shirt like the one Omar has…'

I don't hear the rest of what my sister is saying. Because I already know.

It was Michael.

The Plan

I heard my bedroom door creak open. My shoulders tensed, but it was just Huda. She shut the door quietly behind her.

'Undie folding, hey? You've always had a problem with that.' My sister watched me for a second before picking up two pink pairs off the pile on my bed and shoving them in her pocket. 'I'll be needing these.'

'What happened last night?' I asked her. 'What did she do to you?' I hadn't been able to talk to Huda since she'd jumped out the bathroom window.

My sister rolled her eyes and plonked herself onto my bed. 'Ugh, it was the worst! She told Mr Kostiki I had a fever and it was making me sleepwalk. Then she gave me a lecture for like six hours about how the police could've picked me up and taken me to a kids' home if they'd found me running around in the night without shoes.'

I noticed a bulge under my sister's red school jumper. Huda tapped it. 'It's a special day, Akeal.' She was grinning. And she was also using my name.

'Yeh, a special day to get us both caught by Aunt Amel. C'mon, you'd better get changed and get on with your jobs before she does her check-in.'

'I have something special for the special day.'

Huda wasn't grinning as much anymore. She was still smiling, but I could tell from her eyes that she was sad. So I stopped folding.

'Okay. Tell me. What's so good about today, and what's that weird lump under your uniform?'

Huda swung her legs around to face me and looked around my room. She took a deep breath. And then another.

'Earth to Huda! What's going on?' I threw a pair of undies at her.

'It's my birthday.' She threw them back and hit me in the face.

My eyes widened. We don't celebrate birthdays, but for some reason Huda celebrates hers, and we just go along with it.

'I don't blame you or anyone else for forgetting,' she said with a sigh. 'I know Aunt Amel has everyone stressed out and working all the time. So don't feel bad. I just feel a bit down that Mum and Dad aren't here.'

'I'm sorry for forgetting. You're right, everyone is stressed out, but we shouldn't have forgotten.'

A little pain went through my chest thinking that my sister had spent her ninth birthday feeling sad.

'It's okay. I got us a donut from the canteen today to celebrate.'

Huda pulled a small brown paper bag from under her T-shirt. The donut was squashed and the paper had gone greasy, but this was Huda's birthday. Plus, I was starving.

Huda was smiling again now and licking her lips. 'When I told Mrs Mustafa it was my birthday she gave me an icy pole and a donut for free. I saved it to share with you.'

It was stuff like this that made me like my little sister. She grabbed the donut and ripped it in half. Her fingers looked a bit grubby, but I wasn't going to complain. Not today. She looked at both halves of the donut, and as she passed me the bigger bit, the door swung open.

Suha and Layla never knock – they barge in. Omar and Kholoud followed behind them.

Kholoud closed the door and lifted her finger to her lips. 'Shhh. She's just started watching her favourite soap opera. We don't have much time.'

My older sisters joined me and Huda on the bed while Omar sat on my desk chair. He pulled a phone from his pocket. It was Dad's – the one he'd left behind for us to use as the family phone. I couldn't believe my eyes.

'Oh, no way! How'd you get that?' Huda's mouth was half filled with jam donut.

'Suha and Layla pinched it from her robe pocket when she chucked the robe on the couch,' Omar told us.

'Took ages to make sure she wasn't looking,' Suha chimed in.

I knew what this meant. It meant we could tell Mum and Dad everything.

Kholoud kept her eye on the door. 'Hurry up and call,' she whispered.

Omar scrolled down to Mum's number. Before he hit *dial*, he looked at each of us. 'We're gonna be okay. Once Mum and Dad know, they'll be packing their stuff.' Then he tapped the screen and held the phone to his ear.

We knew numbers overseas took ages to connect sometimes, but there was no connection at all this time. Just three long beeps, and then the phone cut. We could hear it from my bed. Omar swallowed. Then redialled. The same. He redialled again. Three long beeps, then cut.

'Why aren't they answering?' Huda whispered, holding her hands up to her mouth.

My big brother sighed deeply. 'They haven't turned on the international roaming setting. I showed them ten times how to do it before they left.' He closed his eyes and rubbed his forehead with his hand, like he had a headache.

'What does that mean? We can't call them?' Kholoud asked the obvious question we were all thinking.

Omar shook his head.

'What if we used another phone?' I knew the answer before I'd finished asking.

'It won't connect...' Omar paused, and then to make sure we understood, he finished his sentence. 'From any phone.'

Huda jumped off the bed. A small blob of jam from the donut had dribbled onto the front of her jumper.

'There has to be another way to let Mum and Dad know what's going on!'

Omar narrowed his eyes. Suha and Layla shook their heads.

'Yeh Huda, you can just jump on a plane and tell Mum and Dad, then.' Kholoud stood up to leave.

Omar passed the phone to Layla and reminded the twins to put it back exactly where they'd found it. Then he gently opened the door. There was Aunt Amel, with her ear pressed to the door. She stumbled forward a little as it opened. She was cradling baby Raheed, who was fast asleep in her arms.

'Want to tell Mum and Dad how awful I am, do you?' Aunt Amel raised her eyebrows. Her voice shook, and her bottom lip quivered.

None of us kids spoke. There was silence except for Huda's gulp.

'I have tried to help you be the very best you can be. I have tried to show you that you are capable of reaching the stars.' Aunt Amel sniffed and looked at the carpet.

Huda stepped forward.

'You've used us so you can have a holiday! You've treated us like servants!'

I couldn't believe my little sister had said that. I couldn't believe she'd stood up to Aunt Amel.

Aunt Amel snivelled and closed her eyes – almost like she was blocking out what she was hearing.

'Well, Huda,' she said after a lengthy pause, 'since you haven't shown any appreciation for the time I've taken to be here, or for any of the skills and responsibility I've tried to instil in you...'

Aunt Amel was thinking. Then she opened her eyes.

'...you will be no longer be allowed to speak to anyone in this home. Nor they to you. *You* are the cause of all this nonsense.'

'I am *not*!' Huda exploded. 'I've done *everything* you've told me to!'

Tears tracked down my little sister's cheeks, but Aunt Amel ignored her. 'The phone. Give it to me.'

Layla scrambled to give her the phone, and Raheed stirred as Aunt Amel fumbled to reach for it. He opened his eyes and looked at me. Seeing him made me realise just how much I wished I could hold him. And he must have missed me as much as I missed him – because he arched his back and let out a howl. Then he squirmed, twisting to try to wriggle out of Aunt Amel's arms.

'Now look – you've upset your brother.'

Aunt Amel was only looking at Huda. She snatched the phone from Layla's hand and tossed Raheed over her shoulder.

'Little Huda, you need to remember your adab and manners. Your mother raised you better than to speak back to your elders. Now get back to your tasks. All of you.'

Raheed's wails were growing and growing, and Aunt Amel was almost shrieking now herself, trying to shout above the sound. She glared at my little sister before dashing away down the hallway. We watched Raheed reach for us over her shoulder, his face red and wet. But Aunt Amel disappeared into my parents' bedroom and slammed the door shut behind her.

We all just stood there for a moment in the aftermath of Raheed's screams, stunned and quiet. But we knew Aunt Amel would be back soon, and none of us knew what she'd do next.

'C'mon, Layla, we have to make those Anzac biscuits before she asks for her next tea,' Suha whispered to her twin. They walked out of my bedroom.

Kholoud and Omar glanced at Huda, then at me, and followed the twins down the hallway.

Huda alone remained, in the middle of my room, silent. I could see her hands shaking.

'Meet me outside in ten minutes, Akeal. Please.'

☁

Huda stood on the patio with her arms crossed. Her face was still puffy, but there were no more tears.

She yanked me into some bushes so we couldn't be seen. Azalea flowers and bits of twig scratched my face as she yanked me down next to her. A sharp branch dug into my back. Bits of leaves caught in her knotted, messy hair.

'We're getting out of here, Akeal.' She'd used my name. Properly. She was serious.

'Listen, we can't just—'

'I have a plan. A good one. I know where the money is, and I know where Dad stashed our passports. I've been

94

on the aeroplane websites. I watched a show last year where some kids ran away from home. We can do it.'

She was talking really fast, trying to get all the words and information out. She swatted away a leafy branch that hung between our heads.

I sat there, unable to believe what I was hearing. How did she think she could pull it off?

She nodded like she could read my thoughts and then leaned in even closer towards me. 'Trust me, Akeal.'

'Huda, we could get in some serious trouble.'

'Not if we do it perfectly.'

'But we're just kids! No one is going to let us on a plane. All we know about Lebanon is from the cultural projects we had to do in Grade 2! We don't even know where Mum and Dad are in Lebanon!'

'Calm down, calm down. Dad wrote the address on the purple notepad and left it on top of the fridge. I heard him tell Aunt Amel. And guess what?' My sister pulled a torn bit of paper out of her sleeve and giggled. 'I have it right here!'

I felt my eye twitch, but she didn't notice.

'Tell me,' she went on, 'do you want to stay here working like a dog for Aunty Pineapple Head?'

'No, of course—'

'Do you *enjoy* scooping chicken poo every morning in the freezing cold?'

'No, I don't—'

'Do you want to be back with Mum and Dad and away from that horrible fruit brain?'

'Yes, I hate—'

'Well, what are you sooking about?'

I had no answer.

She patted me on the shoulder reassuringly. 'I know you're scared. I know you're worried we might get caught. I am too. But what's the worst thing they can do to us? Like you said, Akeal, we're just kids.'

I swallowed. Hard.

'Okay, so let's pretend for a second that we do go ahead with your plan. You know we don't just buy the tickets at the Sunday market, right? Plus we haven't fixed the computer screen since you knocked it off the table.'

My sister had thrown a potato at me more than a month ago. She'd missed and hit the monitor.

Huda snorted. 'Oh, brother, I might look stupid, but I'm not. I saw how Dad booked his tickets for him and Mum. On the website when we went to the library. And…'

She paused. She was smiling. I hadn't seen her smile like that since before Mum and Dad had left.

'And what?'

'And I know where Aunt Amel hides her handbag. I'm going to use that old avocado's credit card to do it.'

Huda was scary when she was on a mission. I hadn't seen this extreme side to her before.

'So, what do you say? Are you in? Or are you going to stay here and slave away like an animal?'

I wasn't convinced we could pull it off.

'Look, I think it's a good plan, but—'

This was the fifth time she'd cut me off mid-sentence. 'That's good to know that you think that, because I want you to know I'm doing it whether you come or not. I also want to remind you that you're my big brother, and if anything happens to me...you'll be dead meat.'

My mind raced. I had no choice. If Huda went alone, she'd end up kidnapped, arrested or lost in another country. If we went together, I would be able to look out for her. And we might stand a chance of getting to Mum and Dad.

My mouth was dry. 'Okay, fine. Let's do it.' I could barely believe the words had come out of my mouth.

Huda didn't smile. Instead, she raised one eyebrow. Her black pupils gleamed, and my head felt dizzy. I could've sworn I could feel the earth spinning.

'Okay, so, what do we need to do first?' I asked weakly.

'Steal the passports. We can't book tickets without them,' said Huda quickly, licking her lips.

'Where are they? Dad always says he hides them in his special hiding place.'

Huda leaned in closer. She was like a changed person, compared to earlier. She had an energy I hadn't seen since she ate five icy poles in a row at the sports carnival.

'Remember when I nicked those gobstoppers from Kholoud's bag a couple of weeks ago and she went ballistic?' she whispered.

'Yeh, I remember.'

'Well, I hid under Mum and Dad's bed and was gobbling them when Dad came in. He went into their wardrobe, and right at the back, behind all the clothes, he pulled out a black rectangle bag with a handle. I saw him open it and pull out lots of money and some papers. Then I saw him take out a bunch of passports and look at all the pictures until he found his and Mum's.'

Huda must mean Dad's briefcase. I'd seen him with it when he went to important places like the bank. I'd also seen him put money in it after he'd come home from work at the shop. But I didn't know where he hid it. None of us did, before now, but then again none of us had ever thought we needed to know.

'I saw heaps of green money in there, Akeal. Enough for a taxi to the airport, enough to buy snacks, enough to get us to Lebanon and even back again if we needed. Enough for anything we want!'

Huda giggled. She was rubbing her hands together.

'Hang on, we can't steal – especially not from our own parents.'

'We're not *stealing*. We're *borrowing*, to get out of here. Are you telling me Mum and Dad would want us to stay and be treated this way?' There was attitude in my littles sister's voice now.

'Well, no, but we can't just blow their money.'

'Don't worry, we won't.' And Huda quickly changed the subject. 'So, listen, we need to pretend to go to school and then get back inside the house to grab what we need.'

I had to give my sister credit – she had really thought about this.

Huda slapped me roughly on the back a couple of times, as if to say *toughen up*, and rolled out of the bushes like she was some type of superhero. She picked bits of twig off her red jumper as she walked towards the house and stepped up onto the patio. Before she reached the last step, she turned and winked at me.

Turbulence

I don't have the stomach to finish watching my alien versus zombies movie. There's a pain in my belly that keeps coming and going. Every now and then it moves into my chest. When it does, I feel like I can't breathe.

I glance over at Huda. She's still wearing her fancy hijab.

'You don't want to take it off?' I ask my sister.

'Why would I do that?' She scrunches up her nose and tilts her head to the side.

The pain comes back sharper and I cross my arms over my belly.

'Your guts still hurt?'

'A bit.'

'Have some lollies. They're like medicine.' She passes

me the last of her jellybeans, but I shake my head. She shrugs and stuffs them into her pocket.

Mum always knows what to do, no matter what pain I'm in. The last time I had a sore belly she filled up a bucket of hot water and helped me put my feet in. I felt the warmth of the water travel through my toes and then up my legs until it reached my tummy. It made my insides feel snug.

'What do you think Mum and Dad are going to say when we get there?' I ask my sister, who's gazing out the window.

When she turns back to me, I realise just how tired she looks. Her eyes are bloodshot. 'They'll be happy.'

'Reckon they'll believe us when we tell them what Aunt Amel did?'

'Yeh, course they will.' My sister yawns. She doesn't cover her mouth.

'They think Aunt Amel's great, though. Why would they believe us?'

'Coz we're their kids, silly.'

My sister yawns again and stretches out her arms, knocking me in the head.

'Don't worry, Akeal. It's gonna be good. Lebanon is going be so fun. We're gonna see Mum and Dad, plus all the cool stuff we've seen in the photos.'

I'm not sure my sister is right. I'm not sure what will happen when we arrive. I think back to the old photos of Mum and Dad in Lebanon and I just know they're happy like that now. They belong in Lebanon. That's where they're from. But I don't know anything about being Lebanese, other than a few words and some food. I'm fake. Like a try-hard, trying to pretend I'm Lebanese. I don't even know when the right time to serve the coffee is if people come over, or how to have a proper conversation in Arabic without stuttering.

We should've stayed in Melbourne. At home. With our brothers and sisters. Pain stabs through my stomach again. It's hard to breathe.

'Should I ask Martin to get you some warm milk or something?'

I shake my head.

We left them, I think. *We left them there with her.* The thought of my siblings still suffering with Aunt Amel feels like a knife in my guts.

I start to pray. I make a special dua that my brothers and sisters are safe; that they've covered for us somehow, so Aunt Amel hasn't even realised we're missing; and that we'll get through Beirut Airport and make it to Mum and Dad. By the time I'm finished, Huda has fallen asleep. She's sprawled across her tray-table. I pat her head, even though I know she can't feel it.

'I'm sorry, Buds.'

I close my eyes and try to sleep but all I can see are my brothers' and sisters' faces, so instead I stare ahead at the blank screen in front of me.

I'm not sure whether two minutes or two hours go by, but the sound of the pilot clearing her throat over the speaker stirs me.

'We will be experiencing some unexpected turbulence. Please buckle your seatbelts and remain seated.' The pilot's voice sounds twitchy. Huda shifts and opens her eyes.

Martin rushes towards us to make sure we're strapped in and then checks on the other passengers. He isn't smiling, so I know this is serious. He hurries to his spot in the middle of the plane and I see him strap himself in.

Huda's in her own world. I can tell the last week has finally caught up with her. She calmly puts on her earphones and starts browsing for another movie to watch. She pulls her remaining jellybeans out of her pocket and pops several of them into her mouth. I don't think even sugar can help her now.

The plane sails along smoothly, and I'm not sure what the fuss was about. Everyone on the plane carries on chit-chatting and everything feels and looks the same – except for the flashing seatbelt sign. Then the plane jerks a bit and everyone goes silent.

'Whoa!' some man calls out. People think that's funny and laugh. I don't think it's funny, and Huda doesn't care.

Most passengers think the worst is over and keep chatting. A woman unclips her seatbelt and stands up to go to the toilet, but Martin spots her and calls out for her to take her seat. She mumbles something and sits.

I'm not sure if the woman's even done up her seatbelt when the plane jerks a second time. It grumbles hard and shakes like we're in a can of fizzy drink. My head feels light, but I'm still not too worried. Huda isn't either, even though some of her jellybeans have rolled off her tray-table onto the floor. She looks at them, then at me, sticks out her tongue and keeps watching her movie.

Then everything goes into slow motion. The plane almost stops. It drops from the sky and quickly pulls itself back up. I grip my hands to the armrests as the feeling of being on a rollercoaster sweeps over me. My stomach wants to jump out of my mouth, but I tense up to keep all my insides in.

The cabin lights go out and everything goes dark. I tighten my grip on the armrest and in the gloom, Huda looks at me again. But this time I see fear. Her eyes are wide open now. She grabs my hand. The plane drops again, even harder, and shakes wildly from side to side. The overhead lockers burst open and bags and suitcases fall into the aisles. Books and papers and food drop from tray-tables and the laps of passengers. Babies cry and little kids scream. I close my eyes.

This is it. We ran away, and now we won't make it to our parents. Our photo will be on the news. This is what happens when you steal and lie and wag school. Even though Aunt Amel treated us like dirt, we should've just put up with it until Mum and Dad came back. I mean, was it even really that bad? What's wrong with scooping a bit of chicken poo and making a few beds? Now we're going to end up in a million tiny skeleton pieces on some mountain somewhere.

The plane keeps shaking from side to side. It's worse than the scariest theme-park ride imaginable. My head hurts, my necks hurts. I open my eyes and watch as the passengers ahead of me wibble and wobble like jelly. It feels like the plane will tear apart in the sky.

'Akeal.' Huda's voice is low. It's a voice I haven't heard before, because my sister isn't usually scared of anything. I know she's not saying my name because she wants anything. She's saying it because I'm all she has now.

The plane jolts forward again forcefully, and I feel the pressure of being pushed into my seat. No one is talking. No one is laughing. We're all preparing for the worst. Everything is silent except for the rumble of the struggling engines. I hold my breath.

Huda's looking at me. Tears run down her fat cheeks. Snot drips from her runny nose.

'I'm sorry for being a bad sister. You've been the best brother in the world. I hope we can be together in Jannah.'

If the plane doesn't kill me, the pain in my heart will. I wrap my arm around her.

'I won't let you go no matter what,' I say. 'We're strong, Huda. We've been strong since the day we were born. We're gonna be okay.'

My sister lets go of her armrest and grabs me. She's trembling almost as much as the cabin.

'You're the strong one, Akeal. You've always been the bravest.' She tucks herself into my chest and squeezes me.

My heart is about to rip in half when the cabin lights flicker and then turn on. The shaking stops and the plane sails through the sky smoothly once again. Aside from the mess in the cabin and the fear on people's faces, everything has gone back to how it was a few minutes ago. Huda lets go of me.

The pilot clears her throat.

'We apologise for the unexpected turbulence. You may now move about the cabin. Please prepare for the final rubbish collection before landing.'

I turn and look at my sister. She's already wiped her nose and eyes on her sleeve. I can tell because the wet snot is obvious on her jumper. She pushes my arm off her shoulder and elbows me.

'I bet ya thought we were gonna die! You looked like

a scared little prawn on a barbecue!' Huda laughs and starts to shake, pretending she's me.

There's a lot I could say, but I bite my tongue. 'Pick your grubby lollies up off the floor so they don't think we're pigs,' I say instead.

Huda leans over and grabs the jellybeans around her feet.

'Don't eat them,' I say.

Huda grins. 'I won't.'

She flicks her hijab and turns towards the window. I bet she will.

I glance at my hands and they're still trembling. I think about what Huda said. I know she doesn't lie about the important stuff. I think about what I said about us being strong since the day we were born. And I know it's true. I remember the promise I made to Mum, about always looking after my sister.

I grab my hands to stop them shaking, then unclip my seatbelt. Passengers are still picking up their bags and the mess scattered around them. I step over half-eaten dishes of food and headphones as I walk to the front of the plane. I take a deep breath and pull across the thick red curtain that leads to the first-class area.

The seats here are three times as wide as the ones we've been sitting on, and some look like beds. Passengers drink from fancy glass cups and have proper plates to eat off – not aluminium disposable ones like us. It doesn't even smell like our part of the plane. I slowly walk through the huge aisle, scanning each row until I see him. Michael. He's sitting in a pod on his own, flicking through a magazine. He spots me before I have a chance to open my mouth.

'Hey, man! Akeal with the cool shoes!' Michael smiles.

'Hey!' I clear my throat like the captain did before she made her announcement.

'I didn't realise you were on this flight. I would've come and hung out with you.'

'Yeh, my sister told me you were here, so I came to find you.'

Michael tips his head to the side. 'Huh?'

'Yeh, you know, my sister. The one wearing the pink scarf that you tried to rip off her head.'

The smile disappears from Michael's face. Instead, two lines appear between his eyebrows. He puts his magazine down and stands up. I realise he's taller than me.

'Your sister?' His frown gets deeper.

I nod and take another big breath, but I don't let my eyes shift to the floor, as much as they want to.

'My sister. The one who's half your size and did nothing to you.'

Michael's eyes drop to the floor. He doesn't say anything. He bites his lip hard.

'I didn't realise,' he mumbles eventually.

'You didn't realise she was my sister, or you didn't realise that I was a Muslim?' I feel my voice deepen.

'Um…both,' Michael stutters, glancing quickly at me then back at the floor. I feel my fists clench.

'You hurt her. You judged her. You called her names that she isn't. We're not bad people, we're just getting on with stuff like everyone else. Next time you want to pick a fight with a little kid – think twice.'

The words spew out of my mouth. I know I mean them, I just don't know where they came from. I shove my hands into my pockets and take a step back. I'm done. I want to get back to my seat.

Michael's face twitches, and he nods so quickly I barely catch it. 'All right. I get it.'

I'm barely listening as I turn to walk back through the curtains.

'Hey man, listen, sorry if I offended you,' he calls out after me.

I stop and look back. I want to tell him he's only sorry he was caught.

Michael's still frowning, but it's not the same frown as before. I don't know what he's thinking. He's holding one hand out in front of him.

'I said I'm sorry.'

Stealing the Stuff

'Excuse me, sorry to interrupt your television show.' Huda waited for Aunt Amel to pull her eyes away from the screen, but she didn't. She took another sip of tea instead.

It had been two days since Aunt Amel caught us trying to call our parents and blamed Huda for it. She'd been true to her word, refusing to speak to Huda, or to allow any of us to, ever since.

My sister picked at her fingernail, looking smaller than usual for a moment.

'Um…' I cut in, 'do you mind if we walk to school today?'

Aunt Amel paused, the teacup halfway between her

mouth and the small plate on her lap. 'And why do you want to walk? Isn't it a privilege to have me and Omar drop you off?'

Huda shot me a look and I shrugged. I didn't have an answer for that one.

'It is a privilege,' Huda declared. 'We're so lucky that you take us, every single day. It's just that early morning exercise gives us lots of energy, and that means we can learn better and work harder.'

Aunt Amel's eyes skipped between us so many times that her head wobbled.

'Well, *Akeal*,' she said eventually, 'in that case, you may walk to school. But none of that dawdling business, and make sure you fulfil all your responsibilities before you leave!'

Huda grinned and gave me sneaky thumbs up as Aunt Amel lifted the tea to her lips.

'Thank you very much.' Huda curtsied. I didn't know why she'd do that, but then I saw Aunt Amel trying to hide a smile behind her teacup.

Huda took my hand and practically dragged me out of the lounge room.

'Okay, hurry up,' she hissed in the hallway. 'Get your school stuff ready and put on your uniform before she changes her mind.'

I raced to my room and tore off my pyjamas, throwing on my school uniform. We met back in the hall, school-bags in hand. Huda's uniform was creased, her back tracksuit pocket hanging out. I thought she might still have the same ponytail in her hair as when Mum and Dad had left. She looked a mess.

In the kitchen, I opened the bottom drawer of the fridge and two cucumbers rolled towards me. I grabbed them both and threw one to my sister.

'No time for breakfast, or to pack lunch. I have some money left over from Eid. I'll get you a lunch order,' I whispered.

We bolted out the front door, then down the side of the house, ducking between two wheelie bins. Rubbish pick-up wasn't for another day, and Huda instantly pulled her jumper over her face. It was like every single sea creature had died and someone had put them all in our wheelies. The smell was atrocious. I started to choke loudly. Huda glared at me. She pulled her sports jacket from her backpack and chucked it at me, and I tied it around my head.

We both stepped up onto our tippy-toes to peer through the window into my parents' bedroom, which Aunt Amel had taken over.

'We're too short,' groaned Huda. 'Let me stand on your back. I'll be able to check if the coast is clear.'

I got down on all fours and my sister climbed on top of me. I could've sworn she deliberately poked her heels into my back as she popped her head up to the window.

She gasped.

'What is it?' I whispered loudly.

She didn't say anything.

'Is Raheed okay? What can you see?'

Huda climbed down and sat on the concrete next to me. 'You'll never believe it,' she whispered, shaking her head.

I lunged onto the nearest wheelie bin and peered through the window to see for myself. Aunt Amel was on the bed with Raheed, giving him kisses. He wrapped his arms around her neck and gave her a wet kiss on the nose. She threw her head back and chuckled, then rubbed her stomach. Then she lifted Raheed softly into her arms and carried him out of the room. I couldn't hear what she was saying, but I guessed it was time for Raheed to have his breakfast.

I grabbed Huda by the arm and pulled her up onto the wheelie bin too, then pulled the window open. Ripping the jacket from around my head, I dropped it so it landed on top of my schoolbag on the concrete below.

'Go first,' I told my sister. She gripped the edge of the window and kicked her legs in all directions as she wiggled through. I heard a soft thud and knew she'd made it onto the floorboards of the bedroom inside.

I slid my body through too, landing softly on my feet, expecting to see Huda already rifling through the wardrobe for Dad's briefcase. Instead, she stood frozen at the foot of Mum and Dad's bed, sniffling. She didn't have to say anything, because I already knew what she was thinking. I missed them too.

This was the only room Aunt Amel never let us into – even to clean. There were piles of her clothes on the floor, snotty tissues on the bedside tables, and half-drunk cups of tea everywhere. Raheed's toys were scattered about, and the room smelled like an old, wet nappy. This was *not* how Mum and Dad kept the place.

Aunt Amel's footsteps in the hallway shattered my thoughts. Huda's eyes darted around the room in panic. I grabbed her by the arm and threw her under the bed, diving after her just as the door creaked open. I could hear my little brother crying from the kitchen.

Aunt Amel stepped into the room. Had she heard us? Did she know we were there? My mind raced as her bare feet walked towards the bed. Each step was careful and slow, as though she wanted to torture us. I thought I could hear Huda's heart pounding at a million beats a second, then realised it was my own. It was going to explode out of my chest and hit Aunt Amel on the foot. She stopped at the edge of the bed and stood there. Her toes were abnormally long, with little hairs poking out from each one, and her nails were painted purple, care of Kholoud.

I glanced over at my sister. If Aunt Amel pulled us out from under this bed, our lives wouldn't be worth living. Huda's shoulders were up near her neck, like she was a turtle trying to clamber back into her shell. Aunt Amel tapped her foot, as if thinking about what to do next.

All of a sudden, Aunt Amel's arm lunged under the bed, right at me. I wiggled to the side. She lunged again, and I tucked my head into my shoulders to avoid her. The clumsy pineapple wasn't as quick as me. I looked at Huda in elation – it was a small win, but at least it was something. In fact, I may even have chuckled. Very quietly, though. Huda didn't smile back. She widened her eyes at me instead.

Raheed's wailing from the kitchen was getting louder. Aunt Amel went in for the third time, this time feeling around with her long, creepy fingers. I couldn't believe how uncoordinated she was.

Nappy, Huda mouthed at me. She pointed to a pile of nappies next to me, and the penny dropped. I grabbed one and placed it in the path of Aunt Amel's next lunge.

Aunt Amel's hand landed on it. She grunted, then she called to my baby brother, 'I'm coming to change your little poo-poo, my darling!' as she walked out of the room.

My body collapsed into jelly and I shook with silent laughter as I rested on the floorboards for a moment. Huda glared at me. I knew she thought this was my fault.

'All she wanted was a nappy! You could've got us caught with all your laughing and farting around,' she retorted as we climbed out from under the bed.

I had to agree with her. I realised it was best to try to change the subject.

'We'd better hurry up and grab the stuff,' I said. 'Changing Raheed's nappy will only take a few minutes.'

Huda rolled her eyes. 'You find the credit card and I'll get Dad's briefcase,' she said.

Huda tiptoed over to the wardrobe, I spotted Aunt Amel's handbag in the gap between the dressing table and the wall, just where Huda had told me she hid it. The handbag had bits of material flaking off it and looked about a century old. I pulled it open and found Tic Tacs, lollies and chocolates rolling around everywhere inside. A little gold sequin purse with two little clasps sat right at the bottom.

I lifted the purse from the handbag and pulled apart the clasps. There were two pockets on each side, so I unzipped the first and pulled out three hard plastic cards: a gym membership, a pharmacy rewards card, and a library card. I slid them back into their slot.

'Have you found the credit card yet?' my sister hissed.

I shook my head, unzipping the second pocket and pulling another two cards out. The first was Aunt Amel's driver's licence. She looked a lot younger in the photo. The next one was a shiny card with *Mastercard* written on it. Aunt Amel's full name was on it too. *Amel Boogie*. I pushed down a smile and shoved it into my shirt pocket. Returning the other card to its place, I tossed the purse into the handbag and the handbag back into its spot.

Huda was still fumbling in the wardrobe, but next thing I saw her two small, grubby hands poke out of a pile of clothing, holding the handle of Dad's black briefcase. The rest of her popped out too, and she let the briefcase fall to the floor. She looked pleased with herself.

'Open it,' she whispered.

We both squatted beside it. There were two silver latches, one on either end of the briefcase. I pushed both to the side and they clicked open.

'Bismillah,' I whispered.

I lifted open the briefcase and my sister gasped. 'Holy polony!' she whispered.

Inside were bundles of hundred-dollar notes. There were so many that I couldn't even guess how much money it was. Underneath that, I saw seven passports. I knew exactly who they were for. Mum and Dad had been saving for ages to take us kids to visit Lebanon.

Huda and I looked at each other and grinned. 'Let's go,' I said.

Huda grabbed bundles of the money and threw them out the window, onto our backpacks below. I flicked through the passports until I found mine and Huda's, and shoved them into my pocket next to the credit card. Huda ran back to the briefcase and grabbed more money.

'Oi! That's enough!' I said.

'Akeal, what if we end up in Japan or something? We've got to be prepared.'

'Mum and Dad work hard for that cash. We should only take what we need.'

'Yeh yeh, okay.' She raced back to the window and threw the money outside, ignoring me.

Before I shut the briefcase, I slipped an extra passport into my pocket – my little brother Raheed's. I was going to miss him so much. This way, his rosy cheeks and round chubby face would stay close to my heart, no matter what happened.

'Got everything?' my sister asked.

I nodded.

'Good. Chuck it back in the wardrobe and let's get out of here.' Huda was already half out the window.

I did as she suggested. I could hear Raheed laughing again. His bum must be nice and clean. I spent an extra second listening to his giggles before I ran to the window and jumped out onto the concrete outside.

Huda was already snatching the money from the ground, stuffing the bundles into my backpack.

'You're putting all the money in *my* bag?' I whisper-screamed.

'Yeh, I can't risk being caught with it at school. There's a kid in my class who goes through people's bags looking for chips.'

'What if I'm caught with it?'

'You won't be. Trust me. Everyone in your class is boring. Hurry up and let's get out of here.'

She zipped up my bag and shoved it at me. Then she picked up her own backpack and bolted towards the gate. I caught up with her on the street.

'Gimmie the passports and the credit card,' she said. 'I have library class today, so I'll be able to use the computers to book the tickets.'

I took our two passports and the credit card out of my pocket. I wasn't sure this part of her plan was a good one. But before I could say anything, she snatched them out of my hand and shoved them into her own pocket.

'You look stressed out, brother.'

'Are you sure we're doing the right thing?' I asked her.

'Damn tootin' we're doing the right thing. You saw Raheed! He's as happy as ever. Pineapple Head loves him! She won't do anything to hurt him, even if she finds out what we've done.'

She was right. Everything was going well, but I still felt sick. And Huda could tell.

'Listen, buy yourself a nice lunch order and an icy pole today with some of the money in your bag. I took a hundred dollars to do the same. Mum and Dad would want that.'

She gave me a quick pat on the back and then ran ahead of me down the path towards school.

Touchdown in Beirut

Huda squeals and claps her hands together.

'I can't believe it. I can't believe we're actually about to land in Lebanon,' she says.

The silvery sparkles of the Mediterranean Sea startle me when I glance out of the window. It's so shiny and the blue so bright that it's hard to believe what I'm staring at. The sea seems to go on forever, wrapping right across the world's curve.

I pull my eyes away from the window and scan the cabin. Miss Rosetta is sitting up ahead in the middle of the plane, facing us, with her seatbelt on.

'As soon as this plane lands, we gotta bolt,' I tell my sister. She isn't listening, though. She's still staring out the window.

I grab her shoulder. 'Oi, listen.'

Huda jolts and looks at me. She blinks her eyes a couple of times to focus on my face.

'When we land, we have to run. They're not going to let us leave if we don't have Mum and Dad waiting for us at the airport. Grab your stuff as soon as the seatbelt sign is off and follow me.'

The plane lowers itself to the ground and bobs up and down a few times until we're shooting down the runway.

'Get ready,' I say. Huda nods.

The plane begins to slow and then stops. Miss Rosetta unbuckles her seatbelt.

'Welcome to Beirut,' our pilot announces. 'It's a warm, sunny evening, with a high of twenty-nine degrees. Please stay seated until the cabin crew have unlocked the safety doors and the seatbelt sign is switched off. Thank you again for flying with us.'

Huda clutches her backpack to her chest.

DING. The seatbelt sign turns from orange to grey.

Flipping my bag onto my back, I grab my sister's wrist and pull her into the aisle. It's already packed. Almost everyone is standing, trying to reach their bags. There's no time to queue, though; no time to wait our turn.

'Make way, make way! Excuse me!' I push myself forward, holding Huda's wrist tightly.

Mum would be so disappointed with me cutting the queue and pushing past people to get to the front. I elbow my way through until we're almost at the doors of the plane. Then I see Miss Rosetta. And she sees me. She's standing at the exit of the aeroplane, thanking each passenger as they step into the corridor that leads to the airport. Blocking our path to freedom.

'Excuse me, children! Take a seat! You cannot disembark the aircraft without being escorted to your guardian by a member of the flight staff. It's a matter of security.'

I think she's trying to say that someone will have to walk us out to meet our parents.

Miss Rosetta narrows her eyes and presses her lips together. She points to some seats beside her. 'Sit here and wait,' she snaps. Then she looks up and smiles her fake smile at the people behind us. 'Thank you for flying with us. We hope to see you again soon.'

The passengers move past us, someone grumbling something about annoying kids.

Huda tugs hard at my sleeve. 'What do we do? We'll be sent back.'

'Like I said, we need to make a run for it,' I whisper into my sister's ear.

Before either of us can think twice, I charge at the door. Huda charges behind me, screaming like she's going into battle.

Miss Rosetta stops fake smiling and flings her back against the wall of the plane. Her arms fly up, like she's about to be arrested on one of those cop shows. Her mouth dangles open in shock.

My sister's screaming gets even louder as we bolt past her. I'm just grateful she doesn't try to block our path. I hear the beep and static of a walkie-talkie behind us. And then I hear Miss Rosetta screech into it.

'CODE RED. TWO UNACCOMPANIED MINORS HAVE ESCAPED.'

We thunder through the corridor like a couple of elephants who've escaped from the zoo. The sound of running footsteps echoes behind us, but we make it to the end of the tunnel just as glass doors slide open.

I brace myself, like when I'm taking my final big breath before jumping into a pool. We leap through the open door and into the airport. It's as if we've been sucked into a massive wave and spat out into an ocean full of humans. I grab Huda's hand as people shove and push and rush around us. I can barely see my sister, but our outstretched hands cling to each other. The air smells thick, not like Melbourne. Body odour shoots through my nose. The noise from the overhead speakers, buzzers beeping in the background and people talking all around me makes my head spin. I can't make out a word, but I know it's not English.

I grip my sister's hand harder. As hard as I can. But then it happens. The swarms of people are just too much. I feel my sweaty palm begin to slip.

'Akeal! Akeal!' Huda screams. I feel her fingers slide through my hand.

'Don't let go! Please, Akeal!' Even through all the noise, I can hear the desperate crackle in her voice.

But I can't call back to her. Because my hand has already lost hers.

I try to fight back through the crowd, to get back to my sister, but it's like I'm trying to swim in quicksand. The crowd of people has its own plan. I don't know where to go or even which direction will get me out, so I let it swallow me. I let the people push me and shove me until eventually they spit me out, somewhere on the other side.

I collapse on a nearby bench and put my head in my hands. I close my eyes and make a dua.

'Please, Allah, please. Don't let anything bad happen to Huda. I know she's annoying, I know she does irritating stuff, but she'll be better when she grows up a bit. Please, Allah. Please let me find her. Please keep her safe.'

I want to stay strong, but I realise I'm alone too. I squeeze my eyes tight to try to stop the tears.

A voice cuts through my thoughts. 'Akeal?' I know it's Michael from the way he says my name.

I open my eyes and wipe my face with the back of my hand.

'You okay, man?'

I swallow hard. 'I lost my little sister.'

Michael's eyes dart around a bit and he scratches his head.

'We tried so hard to get to Mum and Dad. I tried to look after her, but the crowd was too big.' My throat hurts when I speak.

Michael doesn't say anything. He just stands there. I have nothing to say either. I get up and begin to walk away.

'Isn't that her over there?' Michael points – past the glass doors we hurtled through earlier, past a crowd of people. Huda's bawling, her back to a wall.

I scream my sister's name at the top of my lungs and race towards her. She sees me and stops crying. I move my legs as fast as they can carry me, my only focus getting to my sister. I don't notice the small suitcase lying on the floor. The suitcase that someone left in my way.

My right foot strikes it and I fly into the air. With my backpack still on, I feel like I weigh a hundred kilos as I crash to the ground. My wrist twists beneath the weight of my body, and my head cracks onto the tiled floor. But I don't have time to feel the pain or care about the blood dripping from my forehead – I have to get up and get to

Huda. I use the back of my hand to wipe the blood away and feel it smear across my face.

Huda runs over to me and I grip onto her to help me off the floor. She looks at my head and winces.

'It's okay, it doesn't hurt. I'm all right,' I tell her, even though sharp stabbing pains shoot through my skull.

'I thought I'd be lost forever, Akeal.' Her words come out in hiccups.

'You know I wouldn't leave you. I'll always look after you.' Some blood drips down my head and onto my jumper.

Huda sniffs and nods. 'Here, wipe your head.' She unzips her bag and pulls out a bunch of serviettes with *Dubai* written on them. Then she glances over my shoulder and it's like she's seen a ghost. My sister lifts her arms to head to protect herself. I turn, ready to leap. It's Michael, standing behind me. He has his palms in the air.

'I'm...I'm not gonna hurt you.'

Huda lowers her eyes to the floor and keeps her arms over her head.

'I'm really sorry about what I did to you before.'

My sister doesn't look at him.

I step forward towards Michael to shield her. He gasps when he sees the gash on my forehead, but I don't let it stop me.

'She's raw. You can't blame her.'

Michael bites his lip and nods. 'I get it. I know she must be scared of me. But I am sorry.'

This time I nod. 'It's a start, I suppose.'

I wipe away the blood with one of the thick serviettes. The swarm of passengers begins to break and I catch a glimpse of Miss Rosetta only metres away. A security guard stands with her, scanning the area for us. I grab my sister's hand.

'Run!'

Miss Rosetta spots us and shouts to her sidekick. 'Over there! Grab them!' she calls, pointing and running towards us as we flee. Luckily there are still a bunch of people around, blocking her path.

I pull Huda behind two rubbish bins.

'They're gonna find us,' she pants.

Miss Rosetta and her guard reach the spot where we were just standing. 'Where'd they go?' Miss Rosetta screams at Michael.

Michael glances at us, hiding behind the bins. 'They ran that way!' he says, pointing in the opposite direction.

Miss Rosetta and the security guard scuttle away.

'They said something about jumping out of the bathroom windows!' he calls out after them. He looks at me and smiles.

'Well, who would've thought...' mutters my sister.

'C'mon,' I say. 'We have to get through the big queues before they come back.'

Time to Leave

The sun was rising as I started scooping the chicken poo. A flash lit up the backyard and I glanced at the sky. It was filled with grey clouds, and little drops of rain began to fall.

I saw the lights on at Mr Kostiki's house and the smoke from his chimney. The few times I'd been over to his place, it had been so warm and cosy. He'd let us play with his medals and his cool old-fashioned polaroid camera. But he never let us take any photos, because he said the film was too expensive. One time, he'd offered us Krakus ham sandwiches. Me and Huda had looked at each other, hoping the other one would tell him. It was Huda who finally did.

'Thank you very much, Mr Kostiki. We don't eat porky things.'

I was worried Mr Kostiki would be grumpy because he'd spent ages in the kitchen making them, but instead he shook his head.

'Of course you don't. My apologies. How about peanut butter instead?'

That was when I really started liking Mr Kostiki, but he still scares me just a little.

I put the shovel down and dragged the bins to the road ready for rubbish collection. They smelled even worse than they had the day before. Another flash lit up the yard and rain pelted down hard. I raced for the front verandah, almost slipping on wet mud. Another flash of light. As I climbed the steps, I heard a rattle behind one of Mum's big pot plants by the front door.

'Oi,' Huda hissed.

I looked around, making sure Aunt Amel wasn't watching. She *still* wasn't letting any of us talk to Huda, not since the phone incident. She said it was one thing for Huda to run through the night to Mr Kostiki's house, but another entirely to ruin everyone's holiday by 'reporting mistruths'. None of us had laid eyes on Dad's phone again since.

I darted over to my sister and squatted beside her as the rain poured down.

'I booked the tickets,' she whispered. 'The plane takes off in three hours.'

'Are you serious! Was it complicated? Did you have any trouble?'

'Nah, piece of piss.'

'That's disgusting, Huda.'

'Was easy as a chimpanzee.'

'Okay, well that doesn't make sense.'

'So, what do I pack?'

'Only what you need. Your school backpack – that's small enough to carry on the plane, so we won't have to check our luggage in. That means no toys or games or dolls. Got it? Only the important stuff, like the passports, tickets and a change of clothes.'

'What about my jewellery box?'

'Just make sure you're ready to go in twenty minutes. Meet me by the letterbox.'

'No problem,' said my sister. She sprang up from behind the pot plant and dived towards the wall of the house, pressing her back against it. She flicked her head about to check if the coast was clear and then snuck through the front door like a cat burglar.

I raced inside too, passing the twins in the kitchen, who were already starting on their second batch of choc-chip cookies for the day. I ran straight to my room and slammed the door shut. I grabbed my bag off the floor and shoved in a jacket, a change of undies and some socks. All the money in the bottom of my backpack would keep us going if we needed anything else along the way. Then I heard a sniffle.

'Seems rather odd to be packing clothes into your schoolbag, doesn't it, Akeal?' It was Aunt Amel. She was standing against the wall by the door.

My blood turned to ice.

'Yeh, I have sports class today. My P.E. teacher tells us to bring a change of clothes.' I could feel my breath quickening but reminded myself to stay calm.

'Huh, is that so?'

'Yep.' I controlled the sound of my voice, so it didn't tremble, then I quickly zipped up my bag and looked her straight in the eye.

Aunt Amel stepped over to my desk and ran her finger along my class timetable sticky taped to the wall. 'Let's just have a looksie, shall we? Friday...Friday...does little Akealie have sports class on Friday?'

My mind went blank. I hadn't even been thinking about school and what classes I had on when I'd lied to her.

She skimmed across Friday's lessons, tapping each one with her peacock-blue fingernails. 'Double English, maths, Italian class and...' She lowered her voice. 'Sport.'

'We have athletics carnival coming up, so we gotta

train.' I didn't look at her while I spoke this time, in case she could read my thoughts.

Aunt Amel tilted her head and narrowed her eyes. 'You know, Akoolie, I can't help but feel that you and your little sister are up to something.'

Little beads of sweat began to tickle my forehead. 'We're just working hard to keep the house tidy for you, that's all. I'd better get back to my jobs now, so I can finish in time for school.' I glanced at the door, to give her the hint.

Amel Amel grinned at me. 'I will find out, you know. I always find out.' She glided to the door, then peered over her shoulder at me one more time. 'Always.' She slammed the door behind her.

I felt like collapsing onto my rug, but instead I quickly dressed myself in a singlet, polo-shirt and jumper. I'd wear my school trackies to the airport – no one would notice. I pressed my ear to the door for a moment, to listen for Aunt Amel, then grabbed a pen and paper from my desk. I scrawled a note, scrunched it up, and held it tightly in my fist. Then I slipped my bag onto my back and walked out of my bedroom.

Aunt Amel was nowhere to be seen. I passed Omar in the kitchen, his eyes ringed with dark circles, his skin looking almost yellow. As my older brother yawned, I shoved the note into his hand. *If we don't come home after school, don't worry – and cover for us.*

Huda had insisted we tell the others nothing, in case they tried to stop us, but I couldn't bring myself to leave them all without so much as a note goodbye.

I didn't wait for Omar to react or look at the note. I bolted out the front door and onto the street, where Huda was waiting for me, her head half in our letterbox.

'What are you doing?' I whispered.

'Just checking if Mum and Dad sent us a postcard.'

The air was cold and I could see just how quickly she was breathing from the white smoky clouds that shot out of her mouth, but at least the lightning and rain had stopped.

'Anything?'

'Nup.'

My sister scratched her cheek and I noticed she was wearing my blue mittens I'd bought from the market.

'Hey! Where'd you get those from?' I said, pointing at my mitts.

'I found them.' She paused. 'In Mum and Dad's room.' She knew I knew she was lying. 'Get over it,' she squealed. 'We're about to go see Mum and Dad.'

I rolled my eyes. Typical Huda move.

'I printed off the tickets at the library yesterday,' she continued. 'They're in my bag. I chucked Aunt Amel's credit card in the recycle bin at school to get rid of it. You have the cash, right?'

I gave her a thumbs up.

'Cool. We're good to go.' She grabbed my thumb, squashed it and then shook it around.

I ripped my arm away from her and glanced at my watch: 8:05 a.m. We were still okay for time. My stomach felt tight.

'Let's run to the shops and get a taxi from the taxi rank near the hairdresser,' I said and started to jog.

'That's smart, Akeal. I always knew you were smart.'

We raced up the street, in the opposite direction to school. I checked over my shoulder in case Aunt Amel had followed us. There was no one around but an early-morning dog-walker. If it was any other day, I would've wet my undies thinking we'd be caught and reported to the principal, but today I needed to leave Aunt Amel behind.

We got to the taxi rank just as one taxi drove off and another arrived. I waved to the driver so he'd know we were his next customers. He stared at me and my sister, then looked around to see if there was anyone else with us.

'Act casual,' I whispered to Huda from the side of my mouth as I took a step towards the car. I opened the passenger door.

'Hi there, mister. We need to get to the airport.'

The taxi driver didn't say anything. He just looked at me. He was wearing a turban on his head and had a couple of silver bangles on his wrist.

'Sorry, mister, I said—'

'I heard what you said, kid. I'm not taking two children to the airport without an adult.'

I wasn't expecting him to say no to us. 'But...' I stuttered uselessly.

Huda then shoved me to the side and poked her head into the passenger door. 'You're gonna be in a lot of trouble if you don't, mister.'

The taxi driver shook his head at my sister.

'Our parents and luggage are in that taxi on the way to the international airport.'

She jabbed her finger towards the taxi turning out from the shopping centre and onto the main road.

'You better make it quick so we don't lose them. They said the next driver would follow them. If you leave us here, we're gonna call the cops.'

The taxi driver's eyes widened. Even though his skin was brown like ours, I could tell his cheeks were going red.

I pinched my sister in the rib and tilted my head to say, *Let's get out of here.* She didn't look at me, though. She didn't take her eyes off him.

'All right, get in. But I'm going to charge you for the last two minutes as well.' He muttered something about us wasting his time.

Huda slammed the passenger door shut. 'Get in before he changes his mind,' she hissed from the side of her mouth.

I opened the back door and Huda climbed in, threw her bag on the floor and slid down the seats to make room for me. I jumped in and we both clicked our seatbelts in at the same time. The taxi driver hit the accelerator.

'So, how's your day been so far, mister?' Huda asked him, sounding casual and like they'd been mates for years. She winked at me.

'Fine.'

'Not very busy?' she asked, tilting her head and frowning, as though she was seriously concerned about how his job was going.

He was looking at her in the rear-view mirror now. 'No.'

'Pick up anyone interesting today?'

'No.'

'Okay, mister. I'll let you concentrate on your driving. My dad says it's annoying when I talk to him too much when he's driving.'

'Yes. It is,' said the driver, spinning the wheel as we turned the corner onto the main highway.

Habib

We double-check no one's on our tail and head to an area where we can see long lines of passengers queuing. At the beginning of each line is a person in a light-brown uniform sitting at a little brown desk. There's a big sign above it all that says: *PASSPORT CONTROL*.

Each desk has a few stamps on it, a couple of pens and a computer, and each of the officers wears a serious frown, as they check papers and passports. I wonder if they're specially trained on how to look so serious when they first get the job. Once each passenger's passport is stamped, they're allowed to walk through to the other side to get their luggage. Then to freedom.

We join the end of one of the lines and wait our turn. I pull my school beanie from my backpack and slip it on, over the cut on my forehead. Huda fiddles with the edges of her passport, and the queue moves forward slowly. Very slowly.

'Hooda and Akeaw, what are you doing at the end of the line?' we hear a familiar voice say.

Me and my sister turn around and see Martin beaming at us. We can't help but throw our arms around him. It's so good to see him again.

'I heard a whisper that you two were meant to be escorted through passport control. Do you mind if I do the honours?'

'Oh, yes please!' Huda squeals.

'You'll be waiting here all day otherwise. Follow me.'

I just know Allah answered my prayers.

We move out of the queue and follow Martin. When we reach the front, we get the chance to properly inspect the giant bearded passport officer sitting before us. His muscles are so big he looks like he could star in one of the latest superhero movies – except this man doesn't look like he'd have much fun taking on baddies. He's busy yelling in Arabic at some people in the next queue to stand behind a yellow line. Veins bulge from his forehead, and I see Huda notice she's standing on, not behind, our yellow line and take a little hop backwards.

'Wait here a tick,' Martin says and steps forward.

I think the passport officer is going to yell at Martin for overstepping the yellow line too – or maybe even have him arrested – but instead he smiles. His teeth are yellow.

'Marteen!' says the officer. He stands awkwardly at his little brown desk so he can throw an arm around Martin. Martin looks like a little kid next to him. 'It been so long, my friend.'

Martin leans in close and we catch bits and pieces of his words as he explains we're unaccompanied minors. The officer glances our way and I gulp. His face scares me. His cheeks are covered in stubbly hair, which eventually turns into a thick beard. His dark eyebrows look like someone got a fat permanent marker and drew one line across his forehead.

Martin beckons us over, speaking quickly. 'Okay kids, it's your turn to go through passport control. You're getting VIP service today as unaccompanied minors. But of course Habib here needs to ask you a couple of questions.'

I feel my stomach churn. I can't move. What if he checks our bags? What if he sees all the money?

Huda elbows me in the side. 'Stop looking all pale and weird, like you have something to hide,' she hisses. 'Don't come over till I signal by scratching my bum.'

Huda winks at me and then skips ahead, singing out, 'Sure thing, Martin,' as she does so. I wondered why my sister can't use a normal signal, like scratching her nose or tapping her shoulder.

I try to breathe deeply while Huda is talking to Habib. He's still standing up at his desk, and she's probably the same height as his knee. I don't know how she'll get through this one. She barely even speaks Arabic.

Huda's waving her arms around, like she's telling a story. At first Habibi glares at her, frowning. But then, out of nowhere, he throws back his head and laughs.

Huda slides her bag off her back and offers it to him to check, but he waves it away. Instead, he looks at her passport and then pats her on the head. He asks her a couple of questions, and each time she speaks he laughs. Then he sits back down and takes a lolly out of his shirt pocket. Huda says something and points at me. He takes out another one and hands her both lollies.

Huda scratches her bum.

I don't know what just happened, but I hope we are safe. I also hope I don't spew on the floor in front of Habib. I approach him slowly.

'Luk, come here boy!' He smiles warmly. 'Mafi ahla min ukhtak.'

Huda leans in close. 'He said there's no one cuter than me, Akeal.'

I want to tell her I understand Arabic and speak it better than her gibberish, but Habib is holding my eye.

'Aaaahhhh, you no speak Arabic, boy? No good, no good. Your sister better than you.'

I feel a pang of indignation.

'You look after sister Huda. She good girl. You maybe not good boy.' Then he turns to my sister. 'You eat two lolly. Two! None for him. Okay, give me passport.'

My sister grins as I pass him my passport. He flicks it open and holds it up to my face.

'Why you come here?'

'Just a holiday,' I stutter.

He passes the passport back and pats Huda on the head again.

'Shukran, Uncle Habib,' she says.

'Yallah, enjoy holiday.'

'Thanks, Habib,' Martin echoes Huda. 'See you on the way back.' And we are through.

The three of us march on through the airport, down a flight of escalators and around a corner. I pull my beanie off, and Martin frowns and stops walking. He unties the hanky from around his neck.

'Let me take a look at you,' he says, tilting my chin upwards. He gently dabs his hanky to the gash on my head. 'Looks like it's a graze and not too deep.' He says this calmly, as he gently wipes around my cut. Then he passes me his hanky and points to a little green sign in front of two doors a few metres away. 'Those are the toilets. Give your face a wash and take a breather. You too, Hooda. I'll be waiting right here for you.'

Me and Huda nod and walk over to the toilets. Huda goes into the women's and I swing open the door to the men's. It's quiet and smells like stale air-freshener, but I'm glad it's empty so I can have a few moments to myself.

I walk over to the sink and look at myself in the mirror. Dark rings circle my eyes, and I seem to have lost the cheer in my face. Maybe it's the blood smeared across my face. I look like a serial killer.

I splash my face with water. The gash on my forehead stings, but Martin was right – it's only a graze. I scrub my cheeks and kept flicking water onto my face until the tap turns itself off. Then I comb my hair with wet fingers and dab my face dry with a few paper towels from the dispenser on the wall, wiping off any bits of blood that the water missed. Almost as good as new, but not quite.

I step into the toilet cubicle behind me . . . except there's no toilet. Just a weird oval-shaped thing in the ground. There are two ridges along each side in the shape of feet, and I feel my stomach wobble. I don't know how these things work, and I don't have the guts to learn. Not today anyway. I convince myself I'm not that busting and walk back out to meet Martin.

Huda's already there. She isn't talking, which is strange. I figure she's just had her own situation with the hole in the floor. Martin doesn't notice. He leads us down another escalator.

Huda pokes me. 'Did you see the dunnies in there?' she asks.

'Yeh, they were weird.'

'Did you use one?'

'Nah, didn't know how to.'

Huda gulps. 'Me either. But I tried.'

I can tell Huda wants to tell me more, but I don't ask. I'm glad when we get to an area filled with luggage carousels. Hundreds of people are gathered around waiting for their suitcases.

'What do your bags look like?' Martin asks us as he rolls up his sleeves, ready to pull our non-existent bags off the conveyor belt.

'We only came with our schoolbags,' Huda says.

Martin's brow creases, but before he has a chance to say anything, my sister shrieks. Miss Rosetta and her security guard have caught up to us. She's seized Huda by the shoulder, but my sister wriggles free and lunges onto the conveyor belt of the nearest carousel. I can't believe my eyes.

Huda scrambles across suitcases and luggage, knocking things over left, right and centre. Passengers gasp loudly, and one woman even screams. The security guard and Miss Rosetta dart after my sister, trying to grab her from the ground, but she's too quick. She knocks a couple of suitcases clean off the conveyor belt as she clambers onto the unmoving metal centre of the carousel and stands there crouched, arms out, looking like a ninja.

'Rosetta, what's going on here?' Martin demands loudly.

'Leave my sister alone! Don't hurt her!' I cry.

Huda's back on the conveyor belt, dodging suitcases, Miss Rosetta and the security guard still hot on her tail. The security guard tries to climb onto the carousel, but he fumbles and the top half of his body collapses onto it. His legs drag across the tiled floor as he struggles to find his grip, then eventually he slips off and flops onto the ground. Miss Rosetta glares down at him as he picks himself back up.

'Hooda! Come on, hop down!' Martin calls over all the gasps. He holds up his palm to stop Miss Rosetta and the security guard as they run past him. *I've got this*, he mouths to them.

He turns back to my sister. 'Okay, Hooda, come down so we can sort this out now.'

Huda listens. But instead of just letting the conveyor belt bring her back around to Martin, she turns and starts struggling against it. I shake my head. It would be like trying to run backwards up a downwards-travelling escalator. An escalator covered in luggage. While hundreds

145

of people watched. Huda almost loses her balance, but not quite.

'My job is to make sure you and your brother are safe,' Martin says reassuringly. 'Now please carefully climb off so we can make sure you meet your parents safely.'

Huda hurdles another suitcase and points at Miss Rosetta. 'You won't make me go with that mean one?'

Miss Rosetta's eyes look like they're about to zap lightning bolts at my sister. 'You will be coming straight with me, little girl, and I will be reporting you to the airline for being in breach of—'

'In breach of what? No one's broken any airline rules,' Martin cut in.

'Those children breached security by running through passport control!' She jabs her pointy finger at each of us.

'Actually, I escorted them through.'

Miss Rosetta's face goes the colour of her lipstick. Before she can say anything else, Martin speaks again.

'That's okay, Rosetta. I'll take them straight to processing and stay with them until we're able to contact their parents.'

'Will you send us to kids' jail?' my sister calls out.

Martin shakes his head. 'I promise you I won't.'

Huda looks at me, and I nod. She breathes in and then slowly breathes out. And then she climbs down.

The security guard considers this case closed and wanders away, but Miss Rosetta turns to Martin. 'You had to be the nice one, didn't you, Martin?'

This is the first time I've seen him get upset. I can tell by the way his breathing changes, and how he holds his fingers up to his temples. 'It doesn't hurt to be nice, Rosetta.'

Miss Rosetta steps closer to him, until she's right up in his face. 'Well, I can tell you now that I won't be taking this disrespect lying down...'

Huda nudges me and tilts her head towards the customs exits and, beyond those, the sliding glass doors leading outside.

'We've gotta get out of here.'

I know she's right. There's no way we'll be able to leave the airport when they realise Mum and Dad aren't here to pick us up.

I only wish we could say goodbye to our friend. Me and Huda race away from the baggage area. We pick the *Nothing to Declare* exit, and just as we scurry through the glass doors beyond that, I peek back at Martin one last time. Miss Rosetta is shouting and jabbing her finger at him, but he glances over at us and smiles. I've still got his hanky in my pocket.

On Our Way

We stand on the kerb outside, watching the cars zoom by. Exhaust fumes fill the air, and people pack into minivans like sardines. Heads stick out of windows, suitcases stack onto the roofs of buses or anywhere they can fit, Lebanese music blasts from drivers' radios. Everything moves so quickly. Men shout in Arabic, taxi drivers haggle for prices. Women everywhere wear colourful hijabs. I haven't seen anything like this before, not even at the mosque on Eid.

My heart races. This is it.

The sun blares down and my eyes sting from how bright it is. My skin tingles and itches. It's winter in Melbourne but the middle of summer here in Lebanon.

I glance down at Huda. Her eyes are wide, soaking in all the sights and sounds in front of us. Her face is red and her skin looks wet and sticky.

Huda rips off her dirty jumper. It's has tears, snot and God knows what else on it.

'These things are so Melbourne, man,' she says as she peels it away from her small, chubby body.

She walks over to a bursting bin a couple of metres away and shoves it in.

I laugh and realise I've probably laughed too loud. But I'm excited. I can't believe we've made it all this way to Beirut.

'Okay, time to go see Mum and Dad,' I say.

Huda smiles and nods. She points to a car with a small pop-up sign on its top. 'All those cars are taxis. See?' she tells me.

They're all different types of cars, most of them ancient, but they all have red signs sticking off the top that say *TAXI*. And it looks like they are all driven by really, really old men.

I stretch out my arm and shout, just like I've seen in the movies. 'Taxi!'

Three cars screech to a stop next to us and we run over to the cleanest, newest-looking car. The other two look like something P-platers hoon around in back home.

The grandpa driver in the taxi leans over and speaks through the open window. 'La wein?' he asks in a dry voice and without a smile.

'Dad's note. Gimme the address,' I tell my sister.

Huda shoves the crumpled paper at me. I point to the Arabic words as I pass it over to him.

His glasses sit on the tip of his nose and his lips move as he reads the address. The lines in his face look deep. I wonder if the skin lifts like a flap when he washes his face in the morning.

'Bar Elias, Beqaa...' he mumbles. Then he flicks his head quickly to the side to say *get in*.

I look at my sister. 'That was easy,' she says as I open the back door and climb in.

'Shukran shukran,' I say, trying to sound as Lebanese as possible.

Huda slides into the back seat after me and slams the taxi door shut. I stretch out my arm to grab the seatbelt. Except there isn't one.

Huda's doing the same thing. 'No seatbelts! What if we crash? We'll go flying out the window!' my sister scream-whispers to me.

She's right. But I can't show her I want to freak out too. 'Just put your backpack on your lap. If anything happens, it will act like an airbag,' I tell her, very matter-of-fact.

I know this isn't true – we will definitely go flying through the window.

The taxi driver turns the steering wheel ready to pull away from the airport, but before he takes off, he flicks on the radio. Full blast. A woman's voice singing some fast belly-dancing song booms through the car as he speeds out onto the Beirut streets.

At first, I can't put my finger on what's so strange about the streets. But then it hits me. All the cars are driving on the wrong side of the road. I blink my eyes a few times to get used to it. The early evening sun shining on my grimy, sweaty skin feels so good. Almost like a big warm hug. I smile to myself, thinking it must be Lebanon greeting me. Even though there are no seatbelts, and the taxi driver is weaving in and out of traffic like a maniac on the wrong side of the road, I actually feel safe.

The streets are busy. There are people walking all over the place, and lots of little shops and delis with kids playing out the front. Massive billboards are everywhere, seeming like they should be in Australia except for the Arabic writing. I stick my head out of the speeding taxi's window and take it all in. I could've never imagined Lebanon to be like this. So much of it is shiny and new: huge buildings and clock towers, cafés and shopping strips. Heaps of people look like they're straight out of a fashion magazine, wearing coordinated outfits and carrying bright handbags.

The driver turns into a side street and then into another little road. That's when everything becomes less fancy and I notice the ruined buildings. They look like a huge meteor crashed into them and blew them to smithereens.

Huda nudges me. She's still holding on tightly to her backpack. 'What the heck happened over there?' She nods towards a set of apartments that has the roof and most of the side missing.

I remember Mum and Dad talking about it in sad voices. And I remember reading about it ages ago. It's why Mum and Dad have always said we're lucky to be safe in our home in Australia.

'War,' is all I can say.

The taxi driver seems to hear us over the music, or maybe he sees our faces in the rear-view mirror.

'Big bomb come from plane!' He makes a big sound like an explosion going off, which makes Huda jump. Then he shakes his head in a sad way and shrugs his shoulders as if to say, *What can we do?*

The more we drive, the more we see. More buildings with more holes taken out of them.

We turn back onto a main street and traffic begins to slow. I glance ahead past the taxi driver's head and see the cars all banked up. There are no road lines, but there are four lanes of cars. I notice most drivers don't bother to indicate as they pull out in front of each other. And the beeping all around us begins to give me a headache. Everyone seems to be beeping, all the time, over nothing.

'Why are all the drivers so angry here?' I say to my sister.

'They're not angry. They're just beeping so other drivers know that there's a car close by.'

It takes me a second but then I realise my sister is right. The drivers aren't annoyed – they're honking their horns in little tappy beeps to say, *Hey buddy, beep, I'm here, beep. Let me through, please, beep. Thanks, beep.*

Huda seems to relax a little then, because she takes her backpack off her lap and places it on the seat between us. A note falls from its open front pocket. I pick it up off the floor. It's folded neatly and it has *Huda* scrawled on it in fancy writing.

Huda tries to grab the note out of my hands, and that makes me want to open it. Bad. Leaning away from her and towards the window, I unfold the paper.

I have the evidence. I would have enjoyed the Middle Eastern travel experience, had it not been for my airline travel ban. I told them I couldn't hear the announcements! I know Akeal will look after you. He's a worthy comrade.

Safe journey.

P.S. – The plan is set. Your siblings will join me at 16:00.

Dr K.

I can feel my mouth hanging open but no words come out. Huda speaks before I can.

'Okay, don't be annoyed. I was worried you'd blow it. Although I *did* mean to tell you about this once we were on the plane and I...I kind of got excited and forgot, I suppose.'

'You and Mr Kostiki had another plan going this whole time?' I splutter.

'Well, kind of.'

'Why would you think I'd blow it?'

'Coz you'd have done that face you're doing right now. You'd have walked around sweating and acting strange in front of Aunt Amel. I couldn't risk it. It was enough you worrying about our own mission.' She jabs her finger at my head.

My mind races back to Huda checking the letterbox this morning. It feels like a lifetime ago. 'You've been writing notes to each other?'

'Yeh, every day. Mr Kostiki knows everything. He knew Aunt Amel was fibbing when she told him I was sleepwalking that night I ran to his house.'

'How'd he know?'

'Coz he remembered Mum telling him last year that I'm the only kid who always sleeps right through the night, like a dead person. And also, because he used to be a sleep doctor and he said I didn't show any of the classic signs of somnambulism.'

I can barely understand what she's saying.

'So, anyway, we worked out a plan. You don't need to worry about a thing, Akeaw.'

My sister grabs the note from my hand and stuffs it into the side pocket of her bag. As if that's that. As if I don't have a million questions. But before I can ask a single one of them, she nudges me with her elbow. Her eyes are wide. Like she's seen a ghost from the past.

'Check it out!' She points to a massive yellow-and-red building, with golden arches.

There, on the other side of the world, is McDonald's.

'What the heck?' I say despite myself. 'I thought this place would only have kebabs and sheesh laham.' My tummy rumbles.

Huda leans forward and taps the taxi driver on the shoulder, and not in a polite way. I call tell she's starving too. 'Excuse me, ya zalami? McDonald's, please.'

I like the way she mixes up her Arabic and English.

The taxi driver glances over his shoulder. 'No.'

Huda flinches and turns to me. 'Maybe he didn't understand my Arabic.'

She taps him on the shoulder again.

'Sorry, mister. I mean can we please stop and get a burger and some fries?' She motions her hand to her mouth like she's eating something and pretends to chew.

This time the driver looks at her in the rear-view mirror for what seems like too long. 'No. Not good food.'

Huda blinks her eyes a few times, trying to understand how he could say no.

Then he leans over to the side, keeping one hand on the steering wheel as he rummages through a plastic bag on the front passenger seat.

He finds what he's looking for and passes it to Huda. It's a Lebanese wrap, wrapped in plastic. It looks like the ones Mum sometimes makes me for school.

'You hungry, you eat zis. Better.'

Huda takes the wrap and gently sits back. She looks at me. Then looks at the wrap. And then she slowly takes off the plastic. She stares out the window as McDonald's gradually disappears behind us. Finally, she bites into the wrap. She chews slowly at first, not knowing what to expect.

'Oh, it has labni in it. Yum.' She licks a bit of the thick, white yoghurt off her lip and bites in again. 'And cucumber. Ahhhh, fresh.'

My stomach rumbles so loudly that she actually hears it. She passes the labni-and-cucumber roll over to me. The taxi driver watches us through the rear-view mirror. I can tell from just his eyes that he's smiling.

I take a bite and it tastes like home – just like the rolls Mum makes me at breakfast, or the ones I find in my lunchbox. Sometimes she puts a bit of mint in them too. I chew slowly and remind myself of how good it feels to be cared for. Better than any burger in the world.

The traffic begins to speed up as we approach an inter-section. A man in a soldier's uniform with a big gun and a funny black tilted hat stands in the middle of the road. He's skinny and tall, and he flaps his arms all over the place. He's trying to tell four directions of cars who can go and who needs to stop. But he looks bored, like he's annoyed and really doesn't care. He's not one of those people who love their jobs, I can tell that for sure.

I can also tell that the gun is a rifle because I saw one like it on an African safari show. But this one just dangles from his shoulder down to his knee, like it's an old shopping bag and he has no idea it's even there. He flaps his arm at our taxi, wanting us to hurry up and pass. I wish our taxi driver would go a bit faster, because the last thing I want is to irritate a man with a gun, who hates his job.

As we drive past, Huda pokes out her tongue at the soldier. I choke on my roll and begin to cough.

157

White-and-green bits spit from my mouth and onto the back of the taxi driver's seat. It doesn't help that we're now zooming down the highway with the wind from the open window hitting me in the face.

Huda looks at me and rolls her eyes. 'He would never shoot a kid, Akeal,' she says smugly.

I turn around just in time to see the soldier standing there in the distance as we zoom away. The traffic is banked up all around him, but he's still. Watching us. Our driver turns the corner and the soldier disappears.

Huda knows what's coming before I can speak. 'Oh come on, it was just a bit of fun! Lighten up!' She waves her hand at me as if she's shooing away a fly and looks out the window.

'No, that was really irresponsible. He could've shot us if he'd wanted to.' I hand her back the roll. I don't feel like eating anymore.

'Don't be so dramatic. Soldiers don't just shoot people for no reason! You've gotta do something really bad, like run over his foot.' She takes two more big bites and finishes the roll, but still won't look at me.

'We're not in Australia anymore. We need to respect the customs of this country,' I try to explain to her.

Huda scrunches the gladwrap into a ball and squeezes it in her fist. 'You're boring. You sound like my teacher,' she grumbles.

The taxi driver turns into a little street and pulls the car over. Now I want to yell at my sister because he's going to throw us out for almost getting him killed. He turns around and hands me the envelope with the address on it.

'Wasalna.' He points to a small white house with a brown flat roof across the street. It has two windows at the front, with black metal bars running across them. There's no garden at the front, just the road, but to the side of the house I can see a huge yard with a massive tree that has low-hanging branches. Perfect for climbing.

Huda looks at the house. Then she looks at me.

'What he say?' Her voice is suddenly very high-pitched.

I can't believe what I'm about to tell her.

'He said we've arrived.'

Both of us sit frozen. In only a few steps, we'll be safe and looked after again. And we can tell Mum and Dad everything.

The taxi driver interrupts my thoughts. He's still looking at us. He rubs his thumb into his fingers: *Where's my cash?*

'Oh, you want to be paid! How much?' I unzip my backpack and rummage to the bottom of the bag.

'One hundred thousand lira.'

'*One hundred thousand lira?*' I'm in shock. That's probably all the money we have.

'Just give it to him, Akeal. Who cares, we're here!'

After almost getting shot by the soldier, I don't need the taxi driver to do anything crazy, so I pull out a thick roll of green notes. There are probably one hundred notes held together by a rubber band. I hope he'll accept it as enough.

His eyes bulge when I shove it towards him. His eyebrows are like little arches that jolt up ready to touch the top of his head. I shake the bundle of notes for him to take it. But instead of grabbing the whole thing, he uses two fingers to carefully pull out only one of the notes.

'Enough,' he says.

'Well, that's a bargain! Thanks, mister!' says Huda. She opens the car door and jumps out.

'Shukran very much,' I tell the driver.

'Allah maak,' he says warmly. He smiles. I don't know why, but I feel like giving him a hug.

Meeting Jido and Tayta

I step out of the car and into the little street. Tiny stones and dust fill the air as the taxi drives away. The road is uneven, with potholes and cracks. Huda is ahead of me, standing in the garden to the side of the house. She's looking up at the big tree. She picks something from one of the low-hanging branches and then turns to me, smiling, lifting her hand into the air.

'Mulberries!'

Huda tosses the berry into her mouth and reaches for more, and I notice that the small white house sits on a corner. On one side, beyond the mulberry tree, lies another house. On the other, beyond another small road, green land stretches as far as the eye can see. The green stops when it reaches mountains far in the distance. I've never seen anything like it.

I walk over to take it all in and I notice a small river running a few metres away. It sits lower than the road and I could've easily missed it. I look further up the side street. The narrow river snakes itself up and around through the farmland. I wonder if this is the river my mum told me about – the one she would swim and play in with her brother as a kid.

Before he left, Dad told me his family lives in another town, a long distance from Bar Elias. He explained that the first time he ever came here, he saw two of the most beautiful things he'd ever seen: this town, and Mum.

Huda's voice interrupts my thoughts, but she's not talking to me. I quickly walk the few steps back to the house and into the yard to see what she's doing.

She's sitting on a bench under the mulberry tree with an old man. He's wearing a grey abaya dress with a white keffiyeh over the top of his head. It drapes down past both his ears. He's short and a little stumpy with a big pot belly. He reminds me of an Arab version of Santa Claus, but without the beard. I know I haven't met him before, but at the same time I feel I know him. He sits leaning forward on the bench, resting his hand on a rake. He's tired. I spot a pile of leaves a couple of metres away.

Huda notices me and waves for me to come over. Her legs are too short to reach the ground, and she's swinging them back and forth under the bench. Her hands are tucked under her thighs and her backpack is a few metres away, chucked on the grass. It's open and a pair of doll's legs stick out. I can tell she's comfortable and happy sitting there in the sun with this old man. She always seems to make friends easily with older people.

'Akeal, this hotel is so cute. I met this gramps when I was pinching mulberries off the tree.'

I walk over to the two of them and he looks up at me. His eyes are so familiar.

Huda keeps swinging her legs.

'I can't really understand what he's saying, and he doesn't know what I'm saying either, but I like the guy,' she says.

'As salamu alaykum.' I say hello politely.

'Wa alaykum as salam.' His voice is soft and smooth. It has a kindness to it. It reminds me of my mum's voice. And then it hits me. It's so obvious. His eyes, his voice, his warmth. We're sitting in his garden. He's my mum's dad. He's my jido.

I clear my throat and pull my shoulders back. I can't help but want to impress him. 'Ana ismi Akeal,' I say, putting my hand on chest. Then I point to my sister. 'Haidi ukhti Huda.'

He smiles and nods politely. He doesn't know who we are. Huda has no idea who he is either. We're all silent for a minute, just looking around at the blue sky, the leaves and the garden.

'We should go, Akeal,' Huda says eventually. 'We have to find Mum and Dad.'

I shake my head at my sister. 'We're not going anywhere. This isn't a hotel, Huda. This is exactly where we're meant to be.'

My little sister opens her mouth to speak but stops. She crumples her nose and scrunches up her lips at the same time, almost like fish-lips. The penny is finally dropping.

I lean in and kiss my grandpa on the forehead. His movements are slow, but I can tell he's a bit startled. I suppose I would be too if a random kid came up and kissed me.

'That's our grandpa? This is his house?' whispers Huda, but she points right at him.

Grandpa looks confused and glances around the garden again. He seems to decide he'd better get on with gathering the leaves and leans on the broom to lift himself off the bench.

'Let me help you, jido,' says Huda.

When he hears the word *jido*, my grandpa's eyes narrow for a split second. Then he looks at me in a way he didn't before. He looks at Huda, who is already sweeping the leaves off the path that stretches around the yard.

'Jido?' my grandpa asks. He chuckles.

I stand beside him and put my arm around his shoulder. He's pretty much my height. I always wondered if people shrink when they get older, and now I know the answer. He smells like perfume, but not the type Mum wears and not even close to the aftershave Dad puts on. But it's a strong perfume, so deep it feels thicker than air going into my nose. I like it. I like being next to him. It reminds me of the way the mosque smells on Fridays.

'Imak binti Hend?' he asks.

'Yes, my mum is your daughter Hend.' I nod so hard my head might snap off.

'Min Australia?'

'Yes, we're from Australia.' My cheeks hurt, I'm smiling so much. I want him to know how happy I am.

And then he laughs again. But differently this time. He brings me into his arms. I rest my head on his wide, soft chest. I feel like I'm sailing through the big blue sky on the fluffiest cloud. He pats my head and tells me he's missed me. I don't know how he could have missed me, but I've missed him too. So much.

The quiet doesn't last as long as I'd like, because I feel Huda wrap her arms around the both of us. She's laughing. And Jido is laughing. And then I'm laughing too. We're all laughing but not saying anything. It feels like a dream.

Through chuckles, Jido takes Huda's chin in his hand and looks at her. 'Mitil Hend.'

'Really, Jido? I look like my mum?' she says proudly.

Grandpa has tears in his eyes. He smiles and nods gently.

Then he turns to me. I think he's going to say something special. But he frowns slightly and surprises me by speaking a little English.

'Mum Dad know come?' He points to the sky and then to the floor.

Back to reality.

'Um, not exactly.' I'm sure he doesn't know what *not exactly* means, so I shake my head. He does that squinty-eyed look at me again.

'Well, Jido,' Huda cuts in, 'it's kinda a long story. First we had Pineapple Head come, and then she was super mean and Akeal had to clean chicken poo and I had to scrub the—'

'Okay, okay, Huda,' I say. 'I think we can go into details later.'

Jido is still smiling, but not as much as before. He's silent now. I can tell he knows this isn't a planned trip, but he hugs us again.

'Have you seen Mama and Baba by any chance?' says Huda in a high voice from underneath his armpit.

He pulls away from us and shuffles a few short, slow steps onto the pavement towards the house. Huda and

166

I stand in the yard, not sure what to do. From over his shoulder, Jido waves for us to follow.

I don't want to believe we might see Mum and Dad again. I don't want to be disappointed if they're not here.

He leads us to a wooden door on the side of the house. It looks like it's about one hundred years old, and it creaks as he turns the knobs and swings it open. I can't see much of the room from outside because it's dark inside. I hold my breath and take a step in. My sister clings to me from behind.

Standing in the dark room, with her back to us, is my mum. She's doing the dishes in a little sink. She puts a clean wet plate on the dish rack and reaches for a pot. It's not really a kitchen – just a sink, a tiny stove and a small bench.

My eyes adjust and I glance around the room. There's a bed on one side with someone in it. I know the person isn't Dad, because I can hear them softly snoring. Dad doesn't snore softly. And he's not that thin. Jido sits on the end of the bed and starts to rub the person's feet gently. I see it's an old woman. My grandma. She's lying on her back, a loose white scarf around her head.

Huda tugs at me from behind. I grab her hand and pull her into the room. She squints her eyes to adjust to the light too. And then she sees Mum.

'Mama.' My sister's voice shakes. Tears fall in giant globs from her eyes.

Mum pauses and lifts her head, as though she's not sure what she heard. Then she returns to scrubbing the dishes.

'Mama,' says Huda again, her voice weak. I'm still holding her hand, and I feel her go floppy and worry her knees might buckle.

Mum lifts her head again and slowly turns around. She sees us standing in the light of the door. The pot falls to the floor, the sound clanging loudly through the small room. Mum grips the bench with one hand and clutches the other to her chest. For a moment, she just stands there, without saying a word. She looks more tired than I've ever seen her before, but her eyes are also bigger than I've ever seen.

I think I expected this moment to be different. I think I expected Mum to react like she does when we step in the door after school – smiling and asking us how our day was. Instead, it looks like she's seen a ghost.

Huda and I walk towards her. Mum still doesn't move. My sister still sobs. But despite it all, Huda lifts her arms and touches the hand Mum is holding to her chest.

'Mama, it's me. Huda.'

With that, it's like the spell is broken. Mum falls to the kitchen floor and wraps her arms around us. Huda sobs, Mum holds us, I stand there taking in Mum's warmth, and Jido watches, smiling, from the end of the bed.

Mum pulls away and holds both of our faces in her hands. She shakes her head, confused.

'What are you doing here?'

Before we can answer, she asks another question.

'How did you get here?'

And another.

'Who brought you here?'

And then a million more.

'Where are your brothers and sisters? Is everything okay? Where's Aunt Amel? Did something happen?'

Huda is silent, except for the occasional whimper. A door from the other side of the room creaks open. Even though it's dim, looking up, I know it's my dad.

He rubs his eyes. 'What's all the noise? Are you okay?' Dad hasn't noticed us.

I clear my throat. 'Baba, it's us.'

Dad stands frozen. His eyes dart around to each of us. Then he focuses on Mum but points at us.

'Are they our kids?' he stutters.

Mum nods. Dad's eyes dart back to us and his face bursts into a huge smile as he charges over.

He grabs Huda and picks her up, holding her face to his chest. My sister's legs dangle and flop about as he wraps his arms tightly around her, swinging her around and kissing the top of her head. Then he lowers her to

169

the floor and reaches over to me, pulling me into his and Huda's cuddle. I could hug him forever.

He draws away and gazes at our faces. He's still beaming.

'Dad, we're happy to be here with you but…' I don't know how to say it.

I look over at my mum. I know she already knows it's not good news.

'Tell us what's happened,' she whispers.

'Bad stuff happened,' I say. 'It might still be happening. We had to run away.'

Huda nods and shivers.

'Where are your brothers and sisters? Are they safe?' Mum's words spill from her mouth.

'Yes, we think they're okay, if they kept doing exactly what Aunt Amel wanted after we left. Otherwise, we're not sure.'

The look on both Mum and Dad's faces change.

'What do you mean, *doing exactly what Aunt Amel wanted*?' Dad asks.

Huda finally speaks. 'She made us her servants. She made us clean all day. She doesn't let the twins go to school, so they can bake her cookies and serve her tea. Kholoud is Aunt Amel's personal beautician, and Omar has to drive her around everywhere, even at night.'

Mum's eyes almost pop out of her head. 'Amel? No, she would never—'

'Yes, Mum. She would. And I have proof.'

Huda drops her bag to the floor and rips open the front velcro pocket. She pulls out a bunch of small photos.

'Mr Kostiki and I tried to call you a million times to tell you, but your phone wouldn't work. So Mr Kostiki spied over the fence and took these.'

The flashes. The flashes that I thought were lightning. They were from Mr Kostiki's camera.

Mum makes a small gasping sound when Huda passes the photos to her. She puts her hand over her mouth. Dad gets up and stands beside her, staring at the photos as Mum flicks through them. His eyes look like black marbles about to pop out of his head.

I lean over and take a peek at what they're looking at: Omar slumped over the steering wheel of Dad's car, with Aunt Amel grinning next to him. Me drenched in rain, shovelling chicken poo in the dark. Huda standing on two crates hanging washing on the Hills hoist. Kholoud crying on the verandah, her mascara smeared around her eyes. Suha and Layla tossing empty bags of flour into the recycling bin.

The last photo shows Aunt Amel carrying a green calico bag down the driveway. The bag has a red hand-drawn circle around it. I have to squint to see it – but there's Raheed's little head, poking out.

I have to hand it to Huda – she's made sure Mum and Dad have all the proof they need. No wonder she wasn't worried about them not believing us, when I asked her about it on the plane.

Mum's hands are shaking. 'Aunt Amel made you all do these things?' she whispers.

Huda nods.

'How could she do this?' Mum asks, but I know it's not a question we can answer.

Mum pulls us into her arms again and holds us. Dad keeps flicking through the photos, staring at each one again, his eyebrows creased.

'She carried Raheed around like a sack of potatoes in that shopping bag?' he asks us, shaking his head.

'We saw him from the window before we left. He's okay. Aunt Amel actually likes him,' I say.

'He's the *only* one she likes,' my sister adds.

Mum takes a deep breath. Her eyes are darting back and forth between both of our faces. I can tell she's thinking quickly. She looks up at Dad. He's shaking his head, like he still can't quite believe what he's just seen and heard.

'Need to call them!' Dad suddenly blurts out. 'Where's the phone?' And he bolts out of the room, through the door he just came from.

There's movement from the bed. I glance over and see my grandma has woken up. She says something to Mum, but I can't make out what. Her voice is so soft, so frail, so gentle.

I don't know how Mum hears her question, but she does. 'My children, Mama,' she replies. Then she realises she's spoken English and says it again in Arabic.

Across the dim room, and despite my grandma's deep wrinkles and exhausted eyes, I see a slight smile. She lifts one of her hands, carefully and with what looks like a lot of effort. She wants us to go to her. I've never seen someone so old before; I've never seen someone so sick before. It scares me a little, but I know this is my mum's mum, and I know I love her already. I'd do anything to make her feel better.

Huda doesn't hesitate like me. She walks straight over and rests one of her hands on my grandma's. With her other hand, she holds my grandma's face – just the same as how Mum held us a moment ago. Huda strokes my grandma's cheek.

'Tayta, it's me, Huda,' she whispers.

My grandma looks up at Huda but doesn't say anything.

I stand by the foot of the bed, beside my grandpa. I shift my feet, unsure what to do.

'I'm sorry you're unwell,' Huda tells my grandma. 'I will make dua to Allah that you feel better.'

I wish I'd thought of that line. But as I stand there silently, I start making a dua that she'll get better. Huda leans down and kisses my grandma on the head. Then she gently tucks a few loose grey hairs back into her scarf. I look over at Mum. Tears are streaming down her face.

'This is Akeal, Tayta,' Huda tells our grandma. Then she leans in really close to her ear and whispers something.

Tayta chuckles. I bet Huda said something bad about me. My sister is back to her old tricks. I know it's time to step forward, so I take a deep breath. I touch my tayta's other hand, which is resting on her belly.

'Tayta, ana Akeal.' My grandma moves her head slightly to get a look at me. She smiles. Even though she's wrinkly, tired and sick, I can tell she would have been beautiful when she was younger. She has the same smile as my mum.

She says something, but I can't make out what because it's hard for her to get the words out. Her breaths are short; it's like she's struggling to get air. She begins to cough dryly, wincing as it takes over her body. My tayta is so thin and frail that I worry she might snap.

Mum rushes to the sink and brings her a glass of water. She kneels beside the bed and lifts my tayta's head to help her to take a sip. As the cough settles, Mum strokes her mum's forehead.

I now realise that my mum is the best at everything. She's the best mum. Dad always says she's the best wife. And now I know she's the best daughter.

Outwitted

'Tayta needs to sleep, come on,' Mum says to us.

Mum stands and tells Jido to call for her if he needs anything. Then she follows Dad to the next room.

Huda gazes at my grandma. She softly recites a short surah from the Quran and cups her hands together, lifting them just below her chin to make a prayer.

'Oh Allah, please make Tayta better so we can all pick mulberries together.'

She kisses our grandma on the cheek and then smiles at our grandpa. I do the same, because I'm not sure what else to do.

We follow Mum and close the door behind us. Dad's pacing up and down with Mum's phone in his hand.

Orange curtains hang from the window, and a matching orange quilt is draped over a bed. There's a small bedside table, and an old wooden wardrobe in the corner.

'I've figured out why it wouldn't connect this whole time and fixed the setting,' Dad says. 'But they haven't answered.' He rubs his hands over his head.

Huda butts in. 'That's coz Aunt Amel has your phone, Dad. But it's okay. The kids aren't with her anymore. They're with Mr Kostiki now.'

I stare at Huda. So do Mum and Dad. 'How could you know that, Huda?' Dad asks eventually, his eyebrow raised.

'It was all part of our grand plan,' Huda says proudly.

Our plan?

She has the decency to pause and throw me an apologetic look before she keeps talking.

'My and Mr Kostiki's plan. We didn't want to tell the big kids what we were up to until Akeal and I were in the air – in case they tried to stop us. Plus, you know no one can keep a secret in our house, right? Anyway, once we were safely out of Melbourne, Mr Kostiki was going to the school. To tell the office he needed to speak to Kholoud urgently, because she'd left her favourite purple gel pen at home. That was when he'd fill her in on everything, and then she'd let the others know about our plan, when she got home after school.'

'But what about Aunt Amel?' I spluttered. 'She caught you that time you tried sneaking over to Mr Kostiki's – how would they *all* manage it without her noticing?'

Huda quirked one eyebrow at me. 'Well, brother, at school Mr Kostiki was slipping Kholoud a little bottle of sleeping potion, left over from when he used to work at the sleep clinic.'

Huda chuckles. Mum shoots Dad a worried look. My sister notices and sighs.

'Mum, don't worry. It's perfectly safe and medicinal! Mr Kostiki said it only knocks people out cold for eight hours.' My sister rolls her eyes. 'So, the twins would give Aunt Amel the tea. She'd fall asleep and then BAM!'

Huda pauses. We all wait eagerly for the next part of her explanation.

'And then...?' Dad asks.

'And then the sibs would grab Raheed from her clutches and take off to Mr Kostiki's house, to chillax until you two get back.' Huda points at Mum and Dad.

Mum opens her mouth to say something, but my sister gets in first.

'Let me tell you, though, the best bit is that Pineapple Head – I mean, Aunt Amel – wouldn't even have realised me and Akeal were missing. Or that the sibs were right next door eating pizza and having a movie marathon of Polish cinema. The tea would last till round midnight,

178

and if she woke up then, in the middle of the night, she'd just go back to sleep. She'll still be asleep and clueless *right now!*'

Everyone stays motionless for at least thirty seconds after she finally stops speaking. My sister...I think even if I lived a thousand years, I'd never be able to predict what goes on in that mind of hers.

Mum bites her lip and grabs the phone. 'Okay then, Huda. Let's try calling Jozef.'

Her fingers fumble as she finds his details. She puts the phone to her ear as it begins to ring. I hear a click, and Mr Kostiki's deep, croaky voice down the line. Me and Huda move in closer so we can hear the conversation. Luckily for us, Mr Kostiki always talks really loudly.

'Hello? Hello?'

'Hello, Jozef? It's Hend, from next door.'

'Hello? Who's that?' He's shouting into the phone. 'I'll put my hearing aids in. Wait.'

There's a pause, then a small crash. Then another pause.

'Got them. Glasses next. Where are the darned things? Who is this?'

'Mr Kostiki, it's me, Hend. I think something terrible has happened to the kids.'

'Which kids?'

'Mr Kostiki, my kids.'

'I know that.' He sounds a bit annoyed. He begins to cough. 'Huda and Akeal are fine,' he says once he's recovered. 'Don't go calling Missing Persons about them. They've probably just arrived in Beirut.' He pauses, like he's checking his watch. 'Yes, they should've landed by now.'

Huda can't control herself and screams towards the phone. 'Hi, Mr Kostiki! We miss you!' Mum winces and presses the loudspeaker button.

'Oh, I see you made it,' Mr Kostiki says warmly. 'Well done. I hope it was a smooth flight.'

Mum butts in, her voice the most serious I've ever heard it. 'Mr Kostiki, the other kids. Are they safe?'

'Hend, your older kids are here. They're in my rumpus room.'

Mum drops the phone and it hits me on the side of the head. Huda catches it on the rebound and puts it to her ear. Dad grabs the bedhead, looking like he's about to faint.

'So it all worked out, Mr Kostiki?' Huda screams into the phone.

'Ahhh, yes, young one. The plan was followed through almost to perfection.'

Huda looks at Mum and Dad and narrows her eyes. 'He says they're okay. Relax!' Then she yells into the phone again. 'I'm gonna hang up and video-call you, okay?'

Mr Kostiki doesn't have time to respond, because Huda hangs up, redials and lifts the phone to her face.

He answers on the first ring. All we see is black, though. He's holding the phone to his ear.

'Mr Kostiki, hello! You have to hold the phone in front of you so we can see you.' Huda's still shouting. I guess this is the voice she usually uses around him.

Mr Kostiki holds the phone way too close to his face, so only his chin is on the screen.

'Can we see my brothers and sisters, please, Mr Kostiki? My parents' faces are all scrunchy and worried.'

'All right, all right. Give me a minute.'

We watch as he walks down his dark hallway. His face is lit up by the phone's light. It looks like a creepy head bobbing around without a body.

He opens the door to his rumpus room and lifts the phone higher up – but still facing him.

'We can't see anyone – just your head!' Huda shouts.

Mr Kostiki turns the phone around, and behind a long row of massive sausages hanging from the ceiling are my sisters and brother, awake already, huddled together on his couch.

When they see my and Huda's faces squished up on the screen, they gasp and leap up to crowd around the phone. Kholoud grins, Suha and Layla clap. Omar shakes his head in amazement. He takes the phone from Mr Kostiki.

'You made it! Good on you!' My brother smiles too.

I'm having a really hard time not bursting into tears. We're a family again.

Huda swings the phone around so Mum and Dad can see Omar's glowing face. Mum stares back with wide eyes, tears streaming down her cheeks. Dad leans in close to the phone, so he can be sure of what he's seeing. He takes a big breath.

'Alhamdulillah, you're safe. Is everyone okay?' he asks.

Before Omar can answer, Mr Kostiki cuts in. 'Aahhh, Ibrahim. That's what I meant to clarify when I said the plan went *almost* perfectly.'

'Where is Raheed?' Mum yells into the phone.

There's a long pause. Then Mr Kostiki clears his throat.

'We don't know. The children followed each step of Huda's plan wonderfully. Kholoud met me at the school office, and let the others know what was happening when she came home from school. Omar made Amel a pot of my special sleepy tea. The twins agreed to take it to her in her room, so she didn't become suspicious. But...'

Mum clutches her chest, and I grab her to stop her from falling to the floor.

Mr Kostiki doesn't finish his sentence.

'She was already gone,' Omar tells us. 'And she took Raheed with her.'

The Journey Back Home

My eyelids feel so heavy. They want to close, but I haven't been able to sleep all night, and not just because of Huda's snoring. Raheed is missing. I know the police are out looking for him, and I know Aunt Amel wouldn't hurt him, but I also know that he belongs with us. His family.

I glance over at my sister. Her face is pressed into the pillow, and drool dribbles from her mouth and glistens in the moonlight. The bedroom door opens and Dad comes in, carrying a small bundle of folded clothes. I can tell he's surprised to see me sitting up on the bed, awake already. He opens his suitcase and shoves the clothes inside. Then he zips the suitcase shut and pulls it up onto its wheels. Mum comes in and hands him a small leather bag.

'The passports and tickets are in here,' she whispers.

Dad nods and then turns to me. 'Are you ready?'

'Yes, Baba.'

'Okay, brave boy – grab your bag.'

I can't hear Mum's sob over the sound of Huda's snoring, but I can tell she's crying from the way her shoulders shake in the gloom.

Dad puts his arm around her. 'We're going to find him.'

Mum doesn't say anything, so Dad keeps talking.

'Just focus on your mum. You can't leave her. Huda will be here to help.'

I hear a car pull up outside, and its headlights flash through the open window. We creep into the living room, where Jido and Tayta are still sleeping. I can see the outline of the mulberry tree in the garden. Birds are starting their morning song. It's so warm already that I don't even need to wear a jumper. Dad gives Mum a kiss on the forehead and tucks the small leather bag under his arm. He walks out to the taxi.

By the ancient wooden door, Mum holds my face in her hands. 'You took care of your sister, like you promised you would. Now your dad is going to bring Raheed home.'

My throat hurts. I know if I speak I'll bawl. So I nod.

I kiss my mum's wet cheek, but just as I'm about to follow Dad out the door, my grandma stirs and sits up in her bed.

I run to my grandma and wrap my arms around her. 'I love you so much, Tayta. I'm going to miss you.' I look into her light-brown eyes, then kiss her on the forehead.

'Allah maak, ya ibni.' Her delicate voice is so precious to my ears. I want to remember her calling me *my boy* forever.

Jido softly snores on his side of the bed. I wish I had time to snuggle up beside him and lean into his cosy body.

Instead, I make dua. 'Oh Allah, please let us find Raheed safe and sound. Oh Allah, please help my grandma get better. And please let me come back here really soon. Ameen,' I whisper.

The taxi driver beeps. So I kiss my jido on the head and race out the door.

It feels like deja vu.

'The flight crew would like to welcome you to Melbourne's Tullamarine International Airport. We will be arriving at the gate momentarily. Please remain in your seats with your seatbelt securely fastened until the aircraft has come to a complete stop...'

I open my eyes, expecting to see Huda next to me. But instead I see Dad.

'You okay?' he says. It's been so long since anyone asked me that.

'I'm all right. Just worried about Raheed.'

Dad nods but doesn't say anything.

We get off the plane and clear passport control as quickly as possible, then take the *Nothing to Declare* customs queue and, at last, make it through the arrivals gate. Happy-looking groups of people holding balloons and *welcome home* signs have gathered around the gate. Their eyes are wide, their faces eager, as they await their loved ones' arrival, and I feel a pang in my chest. I imagine me and my siblings gathering like that, one week from now – in some sort of happy parallel universe, where Aunt Amel was the best babysitter ever.

I wish everything had turned out okay. But it hasn't.

I take a deep breath. I'm not sure where we're heading – to the police station or home. Or perhaps we're going to drive around and look for them. I can tell from the lines on Dad's forehead that it's not the right time to ask. I think about my baby brother Raheed's sweet, chubby cheeks for the billionth time. Why did she take him?

Just at that moment, an announcement comes over the loudspeaker. 'Calling remaining passenger, A. Boogie, for flight JFQ 771 to Wellington, departing at 4:20 p.m. Please check in at desk 57, then proceed to gate 14 immediately. We repeat. Please check in for flight JFQ 771 to Wellington, immediately.'

Something in my brain clicks.

Wellington was in our geography test last term. It's the capital of New Zealand...

And that very first morning with Aunt Amel, when we all stood in the kitchen and she gave each of us a task, she said: *'It's not exactly the New Zealand ski trip I've been dying for, nor even the two-day day-spa at Daylesford, but I've always made the best out of any situation...'*

On top of that, she'd listed Raheed's job last: to be her holiday buddy. I'd assumed she meant for her 'holiday' at our house, but now another possibility hits me in the face like six overdue library books. NEW ZEALAND.

And finally... *A. Boogie.* How many parents out in the world could possibly think that was a good name for their child?

I spot a sign pointing to the departures area of the airport, and I start sprinting. I sort of remember my way from when I was here with Huda two and a half days ago.

'Hey! Where are you going?' Dad cries from behind me.

But there's no time to explain. I have to reach desk 57, and I have to reach it now.

People, signs and destination screens flash by me. I run, and I run, and I run...

Finally, there it is. Departures check-in desk 57. With a big screen above it that says: *Flight JFQ 771 to Wellington, departing at 4:20 p.m. GATE 14.*

Dad catches up and grabs hold of me.

'New Zealand!' I pant-scream into his bewildered face. 'Wellington! Holiday buddy! *BOOGERS!*'

'Akeal!' Dad pant-screams back. 'Where are you talking about?'

But I'm not listening. I'm casting my eyes about frantically, because the entire area is packed.

And then... right up the front of the crowd, standing in front of desk number 57 for flight JFQ 771 to Wellington, I spot a woman in an orange hijab holding a baby in a sling.

I beeline straight for her. She's arguing with a man in a crisp white shirt with a hanky around his neck.

'Ma'am,' he is saying to her from his position behind the desk, 'I've already explained to you why you can't bring the infant on the flight.'

'Yes, but it's very important that we go on this holiday. You don't want me to leave my little baby behind, do you?' Aunt Amel says.

Dad's right beside me. He lunges forward, but I hold him back.

'She's not going anywhere,' I tell him.

I swing my backpack around in front of me and unzip the secret pocket on the side, as Aunt Amel half-climbs over the desk and tries to access his computer herself. The airline attendant fends her off in alarm.

'*Excuse me*, ma'am, you cannot board the plane without valid documentation.'

I rezip the secret pocket, feeling like I have pure gold in my hands. I step forward and clear my throat. Aunt Amel glances over her shoulder. She looks very stressed, but her skin is glowing. Almost as if she's just spent two days at a day-spa in Daylesford...

'Hey, Aunty, you might be needing this if you want to get on that plane.'

And I flutter Raheed's passport in my hand before I toss it to my baba.

Afterword: Four Days Later

Huda's face beams at me from the phone screen.

'So, what did Aunt Amel say when the cops got there?' she asks as she fiddles with her neatly plaited ponytails.

'I've already told you this five times!' I can't help but chuckle.

'But tell me again! Please!'

'Okay, okay. She told the police she was taking Raheed for a short break to escape the family trauma he'd experienced over the last week – from us. When that didn't fly, she changed her story.'

'Uh huh?' said Huda eagerly. 'To what?' Even though she knew the answer already.

'Well, she told them she realised she'd trained us kids so well in being self-sufficient that we didn't need her anymore – only Raheed did. So she'd figured she might as well take him someplace she actually wanted to be, for the second week of her "holiday".'

Huda was shaking her head, rolling her eyes and smiling, all at the same time.

'She *did* book return tickets for them both,' I went on, enjoying this too, 'so she really was planning to bring him home again, but the police were still very unimpressed. Not to mention Mum and Dad! And, Huda, can you imagine how she's going to feel when she gets her next credit card bill and sees our flights on there as well as hers and Raheed's…?'

Huda bursts out laughing, like it's the first time she's heard any of this. She's giggling so hard she can barely hold the phone. Hearing her laugh makes me laugh too, even though it wasn't funny four days ago.

Raheed sits on the rug next to my bed, playing with my favourite marbles – the massive bonkers I know he won't be able to swallow. I lean over and stroke his wispy hair.

Huda finally calms down enough so that I can speak again. 'How's everything over there?' I ask.

Huda presses her lips together. Her smiles fades. 'Not good, Akeal.'

My mouth goes dry. 'What's happened? Is Tayta getting worse?'

My sister doesn't answer.

'Hurry up and tell me. Don't hide anything. I can deal with it.' But I'm not sure I can.

Huda closes her eyes and takes a breath. 'Promise me you won't be upset?'

I nod.

'You pinky promise?'

'I said I promise!' I snap.

'Okay, well, it's not good over here…it's *great! Oh my God*, this is, like, the most AMAZING place ever, and Tayta is feeling so much better, and look at my hair – she plaited it for me this morning. About an hour ago, Jido went and bought me a watermelon from some guy pulling a little cart full of these monster melons, and now he's gone to get me baklawa from the little sweet shop down the road, and our cousins came to see me, and I really liked my cousin Heba's cardigan so she took it off and actually *gave it to me*, and then we had running races along the river…'

Huda hops off the bed, still blabbering about all the fun she's having, and opens the door leading to my grandparents' garden. She switches the phone camera off selfie-mode, and through the glaring sunshine and azalea bushes, I see my mum and Tayta sitting on the bench where we sat with Jido only a few days ago.

192

'Habibi, hello!' My mum's smile shines brighter than the Lebanese sun.

She takes the phone from my sister and holds it up to her and Tayta's faces. I pull my eyes away from Mum and notice my tayta's smooth skin. She has a new glow to her cheeks, and a sparkle in her eye.

'Ya ibni, ana mishtaktilak,' she says in her gentle voice.

'I miss you too, Tayta!'

Mum wraps her free arm around Tayta's shoulder. 'She's doing so much better, habibi. I haven't heard her cough once since yesterday.'

She's smiling through teary eyes. I think back to the dua I made by my tayta's bed. I know Allah was listening.

My bedroom door swings open.

'Is that your mum's voice I can hear?' Dad says. He's carrying his mosque-shaped alarm clock. 'Look what I found in the freezer. It's frozen solid.'

He taps his knuckles against it, then pops the clock on my windowsill to thaw.

Dad picks up Raheed and sits beside me on the bed. From the soft look on his face, I can tell he's noticed my tayta's glow too.

Mum kisses Tayta on the cheek and carries the phone with her further into the garden. Huda appears behind her, swinging from one of the big branches on the mulberry tree.

193

'Oi, Akeaw! Wish you were here! This is the best climbing tree ever!' my sister calls to me.

I can only just make out what she's saying, because her mouth is full of mulberries. Even from here, I can see that her face is stained with purple juice. Mum glances up at Huda and laughs.

'It's almost like the more time my mum spends with Huda, the stronger she gets. It's so strange!' Mum tells my dad.

'You want to hear something even stranger?' Dad retorts. 'These kids are keeping this house spotless. I haven't seen one dish in the sink, or an empty toilet roll on the bathroom floor, since we got home.'

Mum's eyebrows jump so high they almost reach her hijab. 'Let's hope it stays that way. Any news on the tickets?'

'Yes, all sorted. The travel agent is sorting out the best deal for us for the next school break.'

I leap off my bed in excitement. 'Next holidays? We're going to Lebanon?!'

Mum and Dad nod.

'We're all finally going on that holiday,' Dad says. 'Together.'

And on both sides of the world at once, Huda and I dance with joy.

Acknowledgements

Although *Huda and Me* is a work of fiction, the parents and siblings in the story are real. They are my family.

Mum and Dad – Hend and Ibrahim – you are the best parents in the world. Thank you for giving me everything I needed in this world. Thank you for putting up with me. Thank you for always being there. You are the most selfless and giving human beings to ever walk this earth.

To my siblings – Omar, Kholoud, Suha, Layla, Akeal and Raheed – you aren't as nice to me as Mum and Dad are, but I guess you're all right. Each of you has made me a better person in your own way. Omar, you are generous. Kholoud, you are kind. Suha, you dress up as Superman and that makes me laugh. Akeal, you should've given me more of your stuff. Layla, I like it when you buy me things. Raheed, you are perfect. We all know the real stories.

K.L. and N.I., my sweet boys, what did I do to deserve you? I wrote this for you, my loves.

Fadey – I've never met anyone like you and I know I never will. Thank you for all the good you've brought into my life.

This book wouldn't have been possible without some truly extraordinary people.

Thank you to Jodie Webster, my publisher, for believing in the manuscript of *Huda and Me*. Thank you for your gentle guidance, suggestions and special kindness. Without you, this story of a little Muslim girl on a mission would still be sitting in a file on my desktop. Thank you, thank you.

Elise Jones, where do I start? As an editor, you embraced the story, guided me and cast magic with letters and words (and snips). As a human, you are the best of them. No one else could have made this book what it is. No amount of thanks will ever be enough.

To Kirsty Murray, my Faber Writing Academy at Allen & Unwin tutor, you inspired me from day one. You believed in me and this book. You answered my million questions and eased my doubts. I'll never forget your advice, encouragement and support.

Huge thanks to the team at Allen & Unwin – you have brought *Huda and Me* to life. Forever professional, always kind, you have all made the process of submission through to publication a pleasure. I am so lucky.

Thank you, Nick Richardson. I remember sitting at a café on Sydney Road in 2014, telling you about this idea I had, about funny memories from my childhood and the naughty stuff I did. You gave me the advice I needed: there needs to be a story. Thanks to you, here it is. Two years earlier, you believed in me as a journo and gave me my first job in the newsroom. You're a special sort of person, Nick.

Obayda Kannouj – there will only ever be two in the club. Cut! We laughed when it was good and we laughed when it was bad. This book wouldn't have happened without you. Thank you for inspiring me, every single day. PLTs 4eva.

To all the little Muslim girls and boys, wherever you are – you can do anything. You are enough. You don't need to change. Close your eyes and choose your own adventure. Now go for it.

Without Allah's blessing, this book would not exist. Alhamdulliah, always.

About the Author

H. Hayek is the second-youngest of seven children, born to Lebanese-Australian parents. She was born in Adelaide, grew up in Perth and now lives in Melbourne. She struggled with reading and writing through her earliest years at school, but knew from the time she was a little girl that she wanted to work with words. After completing a degree in Mass Communication (Journalism & Public Relations) she went on to graduate with a degree in Teaching. She has worked as a primary school teacher in Melbourne's west and as a journalist. But above all, writing stories involving unique kids, with unique backgrounds, has been her passion. H. Hayek enjoys exploring themes of identity – what it means to be Australian, Muslim and Lebanese. She also enjoys being a little bit mischievous.

'A charming, delightful and original story that kept me smiling the whole way through. Hayek has created a cast of unique and memorable characters – from the precocious, funny, daring Huda, to the big-hearted, patient Akeal, to the intriguing Aunt Amel. What I love most about this story is its mischief, its spirit of adventure and its irresistible invitation to young readers to embrace a story that is familiar at times, and wonderfully fresh and new at others.'

RANDA ABDEL-FATTAH

'Big adventure, big laughs and big heart. *Huda and Me* is exactly what #OzMG needs more of. One minute you're laughing out loud and the next you're wiping away a cheeky tear. Hayek delivers everything contemporary middle grade could hope for. Cheeky, hilarious, heartfelt and with an authenticity only #OwnVoices authors can offer, *Huda and Me* will have you on the edge of your aeroplane seat!'

NAT AMOORE